Luv ya Bunches

Luv ya Bunches

LAUREN MYRACLE

Amulet Books
New York

Library of Congress Cataloging-in-Publication Data

Myracle, Lauren, 1969–
Luv ya bunches / by Lauren Myracle.
p. cm.
Summary: Four friends named Katie-Rose, Yasaman, Camilla, and Violet navigate the ups and downs of fifth grade. Told through text messages, blog posts, screenplay, and straight narrative.
ISBN 978-0-8109-4211-0 (Harry N. Abrams, Inc.)
[1. Friendship—Fiction. 2. Schools—Fiction.] I. Title. II. Title: Love ya bunches.
III. Title: Luv ya bunches.
PZ7.M9955Lu 2009
[Fic]—dc22
2009012585

The text in this book is set in 11-point The Serif Light. The display typefaces are Annabelle, Chalet, FMRustlingBranches, RetrofitLight, Shag, and TriplexSans.

Text copyright © 2009 Lauren Myracle
Book design by Maria T. Middleton

Printed and bound in U.S.A.
10 9 8 7 6 5 4 3 2 1

ABRAMS
THE ART OF BOOKS SINCE 1949

115 West 18th Street
New York, NY 10011
www.abramsbooks.com

For the real,

Violet,

Katie-Rose,

Milla,

and **Yasaman.**

Mwah!

To be overcome
by the fragrance of
flowers is a delectable
form of defeat.

—BEVERLEY NICHOLS

The world is big. There are so many people, sprouting up in every house and school and park and mall. Most of them you won't become friends with. Most you'll never even know. But sometimes, if you're lucky, the universe shines down on you, and possibilities grow.

SUNDAY, AUGUST 23

❊ One ❊

Katie-Rose

(Shot from Katie-Rose's sunshine-yellow video camera)

FADE IN:

EXTERIOR KATIE-ROSE'S HOUSE—BACKYARD
SUNDAY AFTERNOON

KATIE-ROSE (off-screen)
Wave at the camera, Max! Say hi!

MAX, a ten-year-old wearing glasses, sits solidly on a

rope hammock, his feet planted on the ground.

MAX

Katie-Rose, I already said hi. I'm not saying hi
again. And why are you filming me?

KATIE-ROSE

(exasperated)

Because. We have gone over this, Max.

Max's expression doesn't change AT ALL. It is freaky
how the boy can be utterly without nerves on such a
nervous-making day.

MAX

Oh. Right. It's our last day of summer, so you're
filming it.

KATIE-ROSE

Not just our last day of summer. Our last day
before *fifth grade*, Max. We'll be fifth graders—
do you not get how BIG this is? And we need

to practice your social skills so you won't be stuffed in a locker, 'kay?

MAX

You've been watching too much Nickelodeon. We don't even have lockers at Rivendell.

KATIE-ROSE

Well, you still need to practice how not to be socially awkward, and how can I give you tips if you don't let me film you?

Max shakes his head. His hair, which is chlorine-bleached and pouffy, is in desperate need of a trim. How is it that boys can't see these things about them-selves? He's even wearing pink argyle socks *pulled straight up*. How can Max not know that pink argyle socks pulled straight up spells W-R-O-N-G?

MAX

Guys don't need social skills, Katie-Rose. We just talk about Pokémon. Or dominoes. Like the elusive reverse domino effect, which I've been working on for a year, and which I still haven't mastered.

KATIE-ROSE

Oh good Lord in heaven, this is worse than I thought.

MAX

Want me to tell you what the elusive reverse domino effect is?

KATIE-ROSE

No.

MAX

It's the opposite of how dominoes normally fall. Instead of each domino falling forward and knocking over the next, a "revermino" is when the dominoes get tripped from the bottom and collapse backward.

KATIE-ROSE's expression can't be seen on the film, as

she's the one behind the camera. Nonetheless, it's a fair assumption that she radiates a complete lack of enthusiasm.

MAX

Like, okay, imagine you're a domino.

KATIE-ROSE

I'm not a domino.

MAX

In a normal setup, the domino behind you would fall forward and knock you over, so that you land on your nose.

KATIE-ROSE

Unless I put my hands out to catch myself. I would put my hands out, Max. Sheesh.

MAX

Only, dominoes don't have hands. But, in a revermino—

Stop talking about dominoes! *Agggg!* You are being SO ANNOYING!!!

KATIE-ROSE SHUTS THE CAMERA OFF.

Lowering it to her side, she marches over to Max on the hammock and shoves his thigh with her hip. This means *scooch*, and Max obeys. Max pretty much always obeys Katie-Rose, because:

a)   Katie-Rose is a bossy-boots;

b)   Katie-Rose could beat him up in less time than it takes to slurp down an Orange Dream Machine Jamba Juice, even though Katie-Rose is tiny; and

c)   Max is just the obeying sort. Or maybe the agreeable sort. Either way, he scoots.

As Katie-Rose wiggles onto the weathered rope cords of the hammock, she says, "Max, lie down. No, over—*No*, your head at *that* end, stupidhead."

"Stupidhead," when Katie-Rose says it, isn't actually intended as an insult. Or not as a *mean* insult, not when she says it to Max. Katie-Rose and Max have been friends since the dawn of time. Friends like that can call each other "stupidhead."

But if *Medusa* called *Katie-Rose* "stupidhead"? That would *not* be fine. In fact, it would be so far from fine that if "fine" were here in Thousand Oaks, California— where Katie-Rose and Medusa live—then the "un-fine" would be way off at the coldest, icebergiest pinnacle of the North Pole. That's how far from fine it would be.

Katie-Rose is anti-Medusa. Medusa, whose real name is Modessa, is equally anti-Katie-Rose. But, lucky them! They both go to Rivendell Elementary School! *They get to see each other every day!!!!!*

Katie-Rose sighs, and the hammock sighs with her, rocking Max off balance.

"Whoa," he says, gripping the sides.

"Sorry," Katie-Rose says. But seriously, she *really* hopes Medusa doesn't end up in Ms. Perez's class. It's bad enough Katie-Rose has to go to school with her. Do they have to be in the same class, too?

Katie-Rose is also afraid she'll slip up and call Modessa "Medusa" to her face one day. Oh, man, that would be bad.

Max jostles to get better situated, and his pink-socked

feet end up inches from Katie-Rose's face. She wrinkles her nose.

"Max?" she says.

"Yes?"

"You need to change socks."

Max flexes his feet. "I do?"

"You do. And, not to be rude, but ..."

Max waits.

Katie-Rose blows air out of her mouth and gazes straight up. The sky is so blue, it's translucent. She'd like to film that sky one day—but not now.

"The thing is, Max, Pokémon is not interesting. To me. Or to any girl at Rivendell except maybe Natalia Totenburg."

"Natalia played Pokémon Battle Revolution for twelve hours straight," Max says admiringly. "She would have played longer, but her mom made her quit."

"And dominoes are *kind of* interesting"—Katie-Rose has seen the complicated courses Max sets up, with twists and turns and sometimes even marbles that roll down chutes to trigger the next part of the formation— "but not to the people who matter."

Max furrows his brow. "I don't know what that means."

Of course you don't, Katie-Rose thinks. She feels defeated already, and only partly because she knows that, really, *all* people matter. But the person who matters to her, the girl she wants to become friends with ... Well, Katie-Rose feels sure Milla wouldn't go all googly-eyed over the elusive-reverse-whatever.

And maybe Katie-Rose isn't worried about Max's social life.

Maybe she's worried about her own.

Her body grows heavy. Max is a good friend, but he's a boy. She wants a friend who's a girl, who she can do girl things with. Fun girl things, not dumb girl things. And who wouldn't snicker if Katie-Rose had unpolished nails, or wore her knit cap pulled down low. After all, shouldn't people be allowed to wear whatever they want? And if someone thinks nail polish is gross and smells like floor wax, is that such a crime?

What Katie-Rose wants is a *real* friend, the kind that lasts forever. And she knows exactly who it should be.

"Camilla Swanson," she says softly.

"Huh?" Max says.

Katie-Rose looks at him, but her mind is elsewhere. She and Milla have been sort-of friends since last year, when they were PE partners. "Yoga with Maggie" was one of their units, and neither of them could prop their knees on their elbows and balance their whole bodies on their hands. That's how it started, with mucho giggling about their failure at the crane pose, and how someone should invent a "toppled egg" pose, which they would both excel at.

Then, after school got out and summer started, Milla and Katie-Rose ended up in Pioneer Camp together. It was a miracle. Katie-Rose had wondered if she'd feel dorky wearing a pioneer dress and apron and scattering corn for the chickens, but with Milla there, it was a blast. They never got together outside of Pioneer Camp, but they did exchange email addies and screen names. Camilla's screen name is MarshMilla. She has an AOL account just like Katie-Rose. Katie-Rose hasn't IMed her yet, but she wants to.

Maybe she will this afternoon. They could talk about school starting, a perfectly legitimate reason to IM. Plus, on the off chance that Milla has forgotten Katie-Rose, IMing her would remind Milla of Katie-Rose's existence.

"Milla has pretty eyes," Max says, startling Katie-Rose. She'd forgotten he was there.

"Yes, Max," she says. She blushes, and doesn't know why, except maybe from wanting something so much that she got lost in her own head. "But you're not supposed to say that."

"Why not?"

"Because it's random. I don't know. Like when we're skateboarding, and you start talking about hexagons, and I have to say, 'Max, I don't need to know that! It's skateboarding time, not math!'"

"Oh," Max says.

But since Max did bring up the issue of pretty eyes, Katie-Rose is curious.

Do I have pretty eyes? she wants to ask.

Max sits up, making the hammock jounce. "Give me the camera. I'll video you."

"Oh, no, that's okay."

"You said you wanted to work on your social skills."

"*Your* social skills. Not mine."

Max's left foot swings over the rope cords and lands on the grass. Once anchored, he grabs Katie-Rose's camera from her hand, which has gone noodley and helpless.

"You can exist without your camera in your hand for five minutes," Max says. "My mom says you're addicted, by the way."

"To my *camera*?" Katie-Rose says, getting a sweaty feeling. She thought Max's mom liked her. All those times Max's mom offered her a cookie, or a Coke, was she secretly thinking that Katie-Rose had a *camera* addiction?

"She says you hide behind it," Max continues.

"Shut up!" Katie-Rose says hotly. She tries to grab her camera back from Max. "That's the dumbest thing I've ever heard, and anyway, how could I? It's a Sony Cyber-shot. The only way I could hide behind it is if I were a mouse, and even then my tail would stick out!"

"Ready?" Max says, pressing the On button.

FADE IN:

EXTERIOR KATIE-ROSE'S HOUSE—BACKYARD—
SUNDAY AFTERNOON

Katie-Rose, a tiny half-Chinese girl with hair in two
high pigtails, scowls and scoots farther back on the
hammock.

KATIE-ROSE

Turn it off.

MAX

(from behind the camera)
So . . . what's your favorite color?

Katie-Rose rolls her eyes.

KATIE-ROSE

Don't ask that. That's boring.

MAX

It is?

KATIE-ROSE

Yes, Max. Milla is not going to come up to me tomorrow and say, "Katie-Rose! Hiiii! What's your favorite color?" *If* she comes up to me at all. Maybe she'll be back with Quin and Modessa. Maybe they're besties again, even though Quin put mud in Milla's chocolate milkshake at Garden Hills Pool.

MAX

Quin put mud in Camilla's milkshake?

KATIE-ROSE

Modessa told her to. Milla told me about it the next day, while we churned butter. She pretended the butter was Quin's head.

MAX

Why would someone put mud in someone's milkshake? You would never put mud in someone's milkshake.

KATIE-ROSE

Of course I wouldn't, cuz I'm nice.

MAX

A *whole* lot nicer than Quin. Even when you're bossy.

Katie-Rose's eyes do something funny that makes her blink. She's not *teary*. That would be ridiculous. And it doesn't have to do with being called bossy, which she's not, anyway. Or maybe sometimes, but only because she has good ideas.

But if her eyes *were* teary, which they're not, it would be because she thinks she's nicer than Quin, too. She knows she is. And she knows in her heart of hearts that she would be a much better best friend to Milla than Quin or Modessa . . . and yet she's worried that she'll go to school tomorrow and everything will be, like, BAM! No toppled-egg jokes. No churning-Quin's-head jokes. Just Milla and Quin and Modessa giggling and whispering and not looking at Katie-Rose at all.

15

TIGHT ZOOM ON KATIE-ROSE'S FACE:

MAX

Katie-Rose... are you *crying*?

Katie-Rose lunges toward Max, and the image goes
herky-jerky.

KATIE-ROSE

Interview *over*.

FADE TO BLACK.

Yasaman

asaman has a secret: She's good at computer stuff. Really *really* good. In July, she took a computer programming class at the Muslim Youth Center, and she learned how to make her own website. Actually, her own *social utility network*, which is a fancy way of saying a place where her girlfriends (one day) could go (one day) and chat and give each other virtual bling and stuff like that.

She didn't have to pay for it or anything. Her *baba* paid for the class, and then Mr. Aslan directed the students to a "safe place for children" called Web Spinners. It's password protected, but Yasaman herself got to create her password. Not Mr. Aslan.

What Yasaman was interested in is what practically every other girl in her computer class was interested in: Facebook. The boys were interested in Flash animation and making stick figures shoot each other. The girls, however, had older sisters or cousins or babysitters who were on Facebook *all the time*, and when Mr. Aslan wasn't hovering about, they'd whisper about creating fake profiles by claiming to be older and in high school.

Not that they ever would. But it sounded so fun: posting comments, sending cupcakes to your friends, updating your status, like, every second.

Yasaman is attending a Hollywood premiere!

Yasaman is meeting Miley Cyrus!

Yasaman is watching the sun set while sipping Turkish tea!

None of those would ever happen except the drinking Turkish tea part, but hey, a girl could dream.

A girl could also turn her dream into reality, which is what Yasaman (and no other girl in her class) managed to do. Not the Miley Cyrus part, but the Facebook part.

Instead of sneaking onto Facebook under false pretenses, Yasaman simply created her own Facebook.

Well . . . kind of.

So far the basic site *exists*, which is a start. The chat room function is enabled, as is the profile function. Meaning, Yasaman's friends could log on and set up their individual profiles if they wanted. They could IM each other and write on each other's walls and send out invites for sleepovers and stuff. Or they could log on to Yasaman's site and just chat. They wouldn't have to set up profiles if they didn't want to. They could work their way up to that gradually.

So, chatting was enabled, and making profiles, and also uploading pictures and videos, even though Yasaman knew that was possibly crossing into dangerous territory. Last week Yasaman's *baba* came across an article in the *New York Times* about girls posting videos of themselves on the web, videos that showed them hitting and kicking each other. His face turned grim.

"Where are their parents when these girls *catfight*?" he said, turning "cat fight" into a verb. "Yasaman, I am proud you don't have friends like this."

Um, I kind of don't have friends, period, Yasaman wanted to say, but she didn't. Why tell her parents that at school she was the weird girl in the headscarf who was always stumbling and dropping her books?

Along the same lines, why tell her parents about her website? It would alarm them for no reason. Anyway, there are no members on her site except herself.

Le sigh, as her cousin, Hulya, would say.

Right now, Yasaman's website is called BlahBlah-SomethingSomething.com. She's trying to come up with something better.

Maybe, if she had friends who wanted to join, they could come up with the perfect name together.

amilla's worry level is going up. This whole Club Panda business that Modessa and Quin are so into? *Ag!* Milla likes pandas, and she likes clubs, but still. There are too many complicating details, and IMing with Quin about it is making her stomach twisty.

A fresh message appears on her computer screen:

○ ○ ○	Chat with Pandalubber
PandaLubber:	i'm not trying to be pushy or anything, camilla. but r u in???????

All those question marks! All that pressure! Could she just not answer?

No. Quin and Modessa must be answered, one way or another. There will be consequences if she doesn't ... and possibly consequences if she does. It's impossible to know with those two. *Ag, ag, ag.*

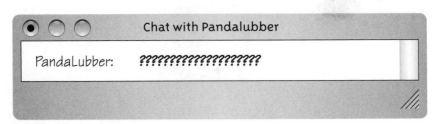

Chat with Pandalubber

PandaLubber: ????????????????????

Milla lifts her fingers over the keyboard. She sighs and starts typing:

Chat with Pandalubber

MarshMilla: i don't know, quin. clubs aren't allowed at rivendell.

PandaLubber: we wouldn't tell anyone. duh! except the girls we let join. modessa says they'll have to go thru intensive training, and even then, we'll only accept the very best.

PandaLubber: since ur top tier already, u'll get to be

	a club panda officer—IF u tell modessa
	soon enuff.
MarshMilla:	what position wld i be?
PandaLubber:	well, modessa wld be president, of course
MarshMilla:	*rolls eyes*
MarshMilla:	of course
PandaLubber:	r u being snotty, milla?
MarshMilla:	no, sorry. go on
PandaLubber:	well, modessa will be prez, i'll be vice-prez, and u'll be secretary.
MarshMilla:	oh
MarshMilla:	what wld i do as secretary?
PandaLubber:	mainly help out with the training. that's a big part of being a panda. oh, and i'm gonna print up a logo for us, won't that be cool? i'll bring u a copy 2morrow.
MarshMilla:	what will we do with the logo?
PandaLubber:	whatever we want. u've gotta think BIG, milla! that's part of having a panda attitude!
PandaLubber:	OMG, BRAINSTORM. a panda attitude = a pandattitude. do u luv, or do u luv?!!

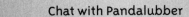

PandaLubber: milla?

PandaLubber: CAMILLA!

MarshMilla: sorry, someone just popped up on my buddy list

PandaLubber: is it modessa?

MarshMilla: no. it's, um . . . katie-rose?

PandaLubber: katie-rose?! super-annoying katie-rose who thinks she knows everything and yet has zero fashion sense?

PandaLubber: what's SHE doing IMing u?

MarshMilla: we were in pioneer camp together. i told u, remember?

MarshMilla: i better c what she wants

PandaLubber: ur so nice. sheesh

MarshMilla: what's wrong with nice?

PandaLubber: a little nice is good. too much nice is bad

PandaLubber: katie-rose is NOT panda material, tho

MarshMilla: yes, quin. gah

PandaLubber: well, i guess i'll go try on my totally cute kilt and make sure it still fits

MarshMilla: the one with the shorts built in? is that what ur wearing 2morrow?

PandaLubber: cuz it's black & white! duh! PANDAS????

MarshMilla: oh. right

PandaLubber: and if u wear black and white too, that
means u've made yr decision.

MarshMilla: i prolly will. there is a 99.9999999999%
chance that i will.

MarshMilla: i just don't wanna get in trouble or hurt
anyone's feelings.

PandaLubber: u can wear all black if u want, or all white.
just don't wear pink or blue or yellow
or orange or red or green or purple. or
BEIGE, not that u ever would.

MarshMilla: what about indigo?

PandaLubber: haha, and no. ANYONE WHO WEARS
COLOR IS **OUT**!!!

four

Violet

V iolet's been in California for only three
days, which is three days more than she'd like.
She didn't want to move here. Who would? Nothing
against California (maybe, she doesn't really know), but
her friends aren't in California. Her house with the front
porch swing isn't in California. Her mom isn't—

She cuts that thought off. Her mom *is* in California,
just not here, which is pretty much the same in terms of
badness. To tell the truth, even worse.

Ever since getting here—just Violet and her dad and
no one else—Violet has felt like she doesn't own her

body anymore. Her *self*. She used to be inside herself, and now . . . she's not. Now it's more like she's *watching* herself, and she's a robot, or a pod person, and she knows she should snap out of it, but she can't.

If her life right now were a poem, it would be so boring. It would go like this:

Violet sits and sits.

Boxes wait to be unpacked.

Violet hates this place.

Her boring life poem is a haiku, which Violet knows because her mom is (was?) a poet. (Does she write poetry, where she is? Is she still a poet even if no more poems flow out of her?) At any rate, Violet's mom taught her about haiku, just as she taught her about prose poetry and sonnets and sestinas.

Violet used to tune her mom out when she went on and on (and on) about poetry. Now Violet wishes she hadn't. But guess what? Too bad, so sad, because Violet isn't a time traveler. She can't go back and change her snotty poetry attitude. As for the future, Violet has no clue whether her mom will go on and on about poetry again.

The term for that, Violet knows, is poetic justice.

"Violet?" her dad calls from downstairs. "Dinner's ready!"

Violet stays motionless on the edge of her new bed with the lumpy mattress, because when her dad says "dinner's ready," it means, "I'm back from In-N-Out Burger," a fast food chain that is apparently really popular in California. If her mom were here and said "dinner's ready," it would have meant, "The chicken I soaked in buttermilk overnight has now been dipped in Parmesan cheese and bread crumbs and baked to golden perfection, so come on down. Let's eat."

But no. It's just Violet and her dad and all these boxes to unpack.

And tomorrow? School, where she won't know a soul.

And the In-N-Out burgers, so wrong-smelling in this already wrong house.

"Violet!" her dad calls. "Got you a chocolate shake—your favorite!"

See Violet cry.

Cry, Violet, cry.

❋ five ❋

Katie-Rose

Chat with MarshMilla

The*rose*knows: milla! hi!!!!!!! ur online! is it ok that i IM'd?

MarshMilla: um, sure

The*rose*knows: i just never have before, is all. but u gave me your screen name, so i figured . . . u know.

The*rose*knows: how r u? r u excited for school?

MarshMilla: kinda, i guess

The*rose*knows: i totally hear u

The*rose*knows: i'm not NERVOUS, exactly. but i know i won't be able to eat dinner tonite.

MarshMilla: me neither. or fall asleep. i'll worry the whole time that our house is going to catch on fire and i'll lose all my stuff.

The*rose*knows: ur worried yr house will catch on fire? why wld that thought even cross your mind?

MarshMilla: well, like becca's did last year

The*rose*knows: milla, becca's house didn't catch on fire. well, ok, it did—but only cuz there was a tornado, and because of the tornado, a lamp got turned over, which *led* to the fire.

MarshMilla: and also her hot tub blew off the back porch and scraped all the shingles from the roof and landed in the field behind her house. what if becca had been in it all that time, u know?

The*rose*knows: but camilla, tornadoes r very rare in california. it is very unlikely that another tornado is going to blow yr house away.

MarshMilla: i know.

The*rose*knows: do u even have a hot tub?

MarshMilla: it's just, i've got everything packed in my backpack for 2morrow. i wld be really sad if anything like that happened. if it burned up *or* blew away.

The*rose*knows: i bought a new backpack. it's purple. but all i put in it was a spiral and some pens.

The*rose*knows: what r u bringing besides that?

MarshMilla: well . . . a bracelet my mom gave me. some shells from when we went to the beach. my bobble-head turtle.

The*rose*knows: tally the turtle! me lub tally! remember when tally fell into the biscuit dough at pioneer camp and mrs. mahoney got sooo mad?

MarshMilla: ha. yeah

The*rose*knows: but i found her and saved her from a fiery death. yay me!

MarshMilla: omg

The*rose*knows: what?

MarshMilla: u just said "fiery death." don't u think that's weird? i never thought about it like that, but ur right—that's exactly what wld have happened if tally had ended up in one of those big ovens!

MarshMilla: a fiery death JUST LIKE I IMAGINED!!!!

The*rose*knows: but . . . tally *didn't* get cooked

MarshMilla: um . . . right. good point

The*rose*knows: i wish i had a tally the turtle. she's so cute

The*rose*knows: not that i'd name her tally, of course!

MarshMilla: she's kinda my good-luck charm. i tell myself that nothing bad can happen to me as long as i've got her.

MarshMilla: stupid, huh?

The*rose*knows: hmmmm. that is very interesting

The*rose*knows: let me ask u this: did u have tally with u when quin put mud in yr milkshake?

MarshMilla: um . . . i'd rather not talk about that, actually

The*rose*knows: just answer my question, yes or no

MarshMilla: no. i didn't have tally that day.

The*rose*knows: well then, that's awesome!!!!

The*rose*knows: not awesome that modessa told quin to put mud in yr milkshake, but awesome cuz it means that maybe tally really *is* yr good-luck charm!

MarshMilla: katie-rose?

The*rose*knows: seriously, just keep tally with u at all times and u'll be safe from fires, tornadoes, *and* mud.

MarshMilla: yeah, ok . . . but cld we stop talking about it?

The*rose*knows: why? cuz it makes u want to churn quin's head up like butter, hahaha?

The*rose*knows: i hope—for yr sake—that you guys aren't in the same class.

The*rose*knows: i'm in ms. perez's class, btw. um . . . r u?

MarshMilla: no, i've got mr. emerson. i *wish* i were in ms. perez's class, tho

The*rose*knows: maybe u can switch! maybe u can get yr moms to have u moved!!!

MarshMilla: won't happen. my mothers r actually glad i'm in a different class from quin and modessa.

The*rose*knows: er . . . i'm sorry. what?

MarshMilla: they say they want me to "branch out."

The*rose*knows: wait a sec. r u telling me that ur in mr. emerson's class and Q & M ARE **BOTH** IN MS. P'S CLASS?!!!!

MarshMilla: sux, doesn't it?

The*rose*knows: omg, i'm in ms. P's class with quin *and* medusa. this is a disaster!!!!!!

MarshMilla: katie-rose! did u just call modessa
MEDUSA?

The*rose*knows: what? no!

MarshMilla: u just called modessa medusa. omg

The*rose*knows: i'm a bad typer. *typist.* c?

The*rose*knows: i wld never call her medusa

MarshMilla: u did it again!

The*rose*knows: no i didn't!—and her parents shouldn't
have given her such a weird name!!!!!!!

The*rose*knows: oh, man, why can't *i* have a good luck
charm like tally? then i wldn't say such
stupid things.

The*rose*knows: PLEASE don't tell, milla. modessa wld *kill*
me. she'd turn me to stone!

MarshMilla: well . . . i won't say anything about that if
u promise not to bring up the mud thing.

The*rose*knows: u said u weren't going to be friends w/
them anymore. r u now trying to erase that
it ever happened?

MarshMilla: when did i say i was going to stop being
friends with them? i never said that!

The*rose*knows: yeah-huh. the day after quin put mud in

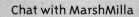

yr milkshake, u were like, "i always go
running back to them, and i don't know
why. but not this time."

MarshMilla: katie-rose . . .

The*rose*knows: what? u did

MarshMilla: listen, i've g2g. i've gotta plan my outfit

The*rose*knows: for school tomorrow? ur planning an outfit?!!

MarshMilla: um . . . yeah?

The*rose*knows: crud. does that mean i'm supposed to plan
an outfit?

MarshMilla: bye, katie-rose

The*rose*knows: omigosh omigosh omigosh, i *never* think
about things like that. they never even
cross my—

The*rose*knows: ooo! i know!!!! i have a totally awesometatiousful tie-dye that's purple and blue
swirled. wld that be good? it's got yellow
in it, too, and a teeny bit of pink. It's
basically a rainbow explosion, haha.

The*rose*knows: milla?

The*rose*knows: did u sign off?

The*rose*knows: well, ok. um . . . bye! c u 2morrow!!!!!

Six

Yasaman

WELCOME TO BLAHBLAHSOMETHINGSOMETHING.COM!
Yasaman types.

No, that's no good, she thinks. It needs color. It needs flair! It needs something to make it *Yasaman* instead of blah...even if the outside world sees the two as one and the same.

Welcome to BlahBlahSomethingSomething.com!

Slightly better. The name's still horrible, but the font is fun and the orange is much more inviting than black. Yasaman loves the color orange—it tickles her nose with tangerines and Pez and gleaming plump pumpkins. She also feels sorry for the color orange, because no one ever says "orange" when asked their favorite color. They say "blue," usually. Blue, blue, blue.

Blue's nice, but it isn't the only color out there.

From here, you can start your own blog! You can share your thoughts and dreams with your friends and let the world know who you really are!

Yasaman twists a chunk of long dark hair around her finger and brings the end to her mouth. Maybe she should delete the "with your friends" part, as she has no friends?

You can share your thoughts and dreams and let the world know who you really are!

Yes. Better. She wants to take the next step and go for it—start sharing her thoughts and dreams—but her brain has locked up. Everything she considers sounds stupid.

So? she argues with herself. *It's not like anyone's going to read it, anyway.* She pulls her hair out of her mouth. Her fingers hover above the keyboard. *You don't have to be brilliant,* she tells herself. *You don't have to be witty. You can say whatever you want.*

First she has to name her journal entry. So, okay:

Pre-School Jitters

No, that makes it sound as if she's three and about to start actual *preschool*. Her little sister, Nigar, is about to start preschool, but Nigar has no jitters whatsoever. She's so proud of her Hello Kitty lunch box that she sleeps with it.

Okay, try again:

School Starts TOMORROW!!!!

That's nice and simple and relatively un-stupid. Excellent. *Now go on and actually write something*, Yasaman tells herself.

~~Hi! Yasaman here!~~ *Aaaaaargh*, this is ridiculous. NO MORE DELETING!!!

Deep breath. Shoulders back. Three, two, one … *type*.

This is MY blog and I can say whatever I want. Nobody cares.

Things about me:

I like frogs

I love books

I love movies, too, but I'm not allowed to see very many

~~sometimes I worry that nobody likes me~~

Yasaman's index finger stays on the Delete key longer than it needs to. Her stomach is an elevator of sadness going down, down, down, and it catches her by surprise. It shouldn't, but it does.

She swivels away from her laptop and goes downstairs. She takes the portable phone from its base and punches in her cousin's number. As the call goes through, she pit-pats quietly back upstairs, returns to her room, and pulls the door almost closed.

"Hulya?" she says. "Hi!"

"Yaz!" Hulya says. "Waddup, cuz? Keeping it real?"

Yasaman grins, because Hulya only talks this way when no one else is around. To Yasaman, she'll say, "Give me some knuckles" or "Yo yo yo," but to their elderly *büyükbaba* and *büyükanne* and their gazillion of *halanin* and *amcanin*, it's "Yes, ma'am, no sir" all the way.

"Um, yeah, I guess I'm keeping it real," Yasaman says. She grips the phone. "School starts tomorrow."

"Yah, I know," Hulya says. "My friend Chrissy? She's insane. She's planning this whole sneak attack on Joseph Terrico, who we call Jellico. She is boy crazy with a capital *boy*, I'm telling ya. She's the total ditzy blonde—I love her. Only she's smart under her ditziness. She *does* have brains, but she'd rather tie a pillow to her tummy and have pretend sumo wrestler fights, ya know?"

Yasaman marvels at the way Hulya's words spill out of her like jelly beans. She also marvels at this *Chrissy* person, whom she envisions as blonde and manic and pillow-huge, bouncing into people's stomachs.

"But even when she's sumo wrestling, she blabbers about boys," Hulya says. "She says she's got 'boy crazy' in her genes. Chrissy's older sister, Angela? She just started college—somewhere in the south, maybe Georgia?—and apparently she's dating an entire fraternity. Can you believe it?"

Yasaman opens her mouth, but before she can reply, Hulya jumps back in. "But not in a slutty way. I'm friends with Angela on Facebook, and she's just as adorable as Chrissy and not skanky at all. Oh! But their aunt? *She's a pole dancer*, Yaz. Can you believe it?"

Yasaman is slightly breathless just from listening to Hulya's spew. "You're Facebook friends with a college girl?"

"Oh, on Facebook you're friends with everybody," Hulya says breezily.

Yasaman hears clicking keyboard sounds. She realizes Hulya is probably on Facebook right this second.

Sure enough, Hulya says, "I'm sending Chrissy a Black Forest cupcake with a heart on it right now, to wish her luck with Jellico. Want me to add a message from you?"

"Wouldn't that be weird? She doesn't even know me."

"Well, I don't technically know Chrissy's sis, Angela, but I've sent *her* cupcakes." She giggles. "But you're probably right. A fifth grader on Facebook would pretty much ruin the vibe."

Yasaman's shame seeps through her pores. It's official: she never should have called her über-peppy, über-popular, über-confident cousin.

"Hey, check it out," Hulya says, as if Yasaman is there looking over her shoulder. "I just got a friend request from this absolute sweetheart I met at the mall. Adorkable— works at Orange Julius, wears a paper hat—but still."

Yasaman hears a single, purposeful click.

"There. Done." Hulya giggles some more. "Omigod, I have a hundred and twenty-two friends now. That kills me."

It kills me, too, Yasaman thinks. One hundred and twenty-two friends, all sending each other cupcakes and *kawaii*-ness (which means "cuteness" in Japanese) and real live baby seals, although Hulya explained that no, a real live seal doesn't arrive on your doorstep. If you accept a baby seal from someone, that just meant you agree to help feed it. Or something.

"Yaz, sweetie, I gotta split," Hulya says. *Tap tap tap* go her fingers on her keyboard. "But I said 'hey' to Chrissy for you. She says 'hey' back, and to tell your mom to hire her as a babysitter. She's trying to save money for a plane ticket to visit her sis at college."

Hulya knows how unlikely that is. If someone needs to take care of Nigar, it'll be Yasaman, and if someone needs to take care of Yasaman—or not "take care" of her, but be there just in case—then it'll be Hulya or one of their aunties. That's just the way it works in Muslim families.

But Yasaman sighs and says, "Sure."

"Awesome," Hulya says. "Have a fab first day of fifth grade! Knock 'em dead!"

The line goes quiet. Yasaman lowers the phone. She

looks at it—so black and lifeless without Hulya's chirpy voice percolating out of it—then punches the Off button.

She goes to her laptop and finishes her blog entry in a desperate burst of peppiness:

> Oh, and I LOVE orange and I LOVE school and I just
> know this is going to be the best year ever!!!

MONDAY, AUGUST 24

❋ Seven ❋

Katie-Rose

(Shot from Katie-Rose's sunshine-yellow video camera)

FADE IN:

INTERIOR KATIE-ROSE'S HOUSE—KITCHEN—
TUESDAY MORNING

Katie-Rose's brothers are wolfing down their Cap'n
Crunch. CHARLIE, an eighth grader, has their mom's
fair coloring and sandy brown hair. SAM, who's
starting sixth grade, has dark hair like their Chinese

dad. In the California school system, elementary school ends after fifth grade and middle school starts in sixth, which means that for the first time in Katie-Rose's life, she won't be at school with either of her brothers.

CHARLIE

(mid-sentence, his mouth full)

—or I'll throw it out the window. I mean it, Katie-Rose. Turn it off.

KATIE-ROSE (off-screen)

One piece of advice, that's all I want. You're supposed to look out for me.

CHARLIE

(snorting)

Fine. Free advice: Get a new personality.

KATIE-ROSE (off-screen)

Mo-o-om ... Charlie's being mean.

CAMERA PANS TO KATIE-ROSE'S MOM, WHO'S AT
THE SINK WASHING DISHES

KATIE-ROSE'S MOM

Charlie, don't be mean to your sister. I think it's
terrific she's trying to reinvent herself. And
Katie-Rose, put down your camera and eat your
cereal.

KATIE-ROSE (off-screen)

You think it's terrific I'm "reinventing" myself?
(beat)
You think I need to be *reinvented*?!

KATIE-ROSE'S MOM

(wincing)
No! Bun-bun, *no*. I just meant . . .

KATIE-ROSE (off-screen)

You just meant *what*?

Sam grabs the video camera from Katie-Rose.

KATIE-ROSE

Hey!

CLOSE-UP ON KATIE-ROSE.

She's wearing her colorful tie-dye. Her hair is up in funny little pigtails, and her cheeks are as pink as the swirls in her shirt.

SAM (off-screen)

Remember when you were, like, five? And you'd just started kindergarten?

KATIE-ROSE

Give me my camera.

SAM (off-screen)

And everybody got you confused with that girl Felicia. Remember?

Katie-Rose holds her hand out, her dark eyes furious.

KATIE-ROSE

Now, Sam.

SAM (off-screen)

Because you're both Chinese. But then they realized you were the one always bossing people around and messing up their games.

KATIE-ROSE

Not true. Shut up.

SAM (off-screen)

(laughing)

And one time Felicia walked by some guys building a fort in the sand, and they were like, "Don't come over here! Go away!" Then they realized it wasn't you and said, "Oh, sorry, Felicia. Thought you were Katie-Rose."

Katie-Rose lunges for Sam and tips over her bowl of Cap'n Crunch. Milk and soggy cereal bits swim over the table and soak Katie-Rose's tie-dye.

SAM

(laughing harder)

Smooth, Katie-Rose.

KATIE-ROSE'S MOM (off-screen)

Oh, sweetie, your shirt!

The images blur and bounce. Under the overlapping voices of her mom telling her to go change and her brothers saying things like, "Yeah, change into a normal human being," Katie-Rose can be heard breathing hard.

KATIE-ROSE (off-screen)

Thanks, everybody. Thanks so much for getting my day off to such a great start.

Finally, she finds the Off button. She punches it.

FADE TO BLACK.

❈ Eight ❈

illa hardly notices as her mom Abigail leans over from the driver's seat and gives her a kiss.

"Good luck, have fun, be kind," Mom Abigail says. "Mom Joyce'll pick you up, 'kay?"

Milla nods. She hasn't been here, at the actual physical building of Rivendell, in three months, and for some reason it's surprising how *real* it is. The building sat vacant all summer long while life spun on, and now kids are mounting the stairs, laughing and high-fiving and hip-bumping each other.

Anxiety bubbles in Milla's stomach.

"This is when you say, 'Okay, Mom,' and get out of the car," Mom Abigail says.

Milla doesn't see Quin or Medusa. *Ack—Modessa!*

Please don't let me slip up and use Katie-Rose's nickname for Modessa, she prays.

(It *is* funny, though.)

Mom Abigail clears her throat. "But in order to get out of the car, you actually have to open the door, swing your legs out, plant your feet on the pavement . . ."

Milla swivels her head toward her mom. "Huh?"

Mom Abigail chuckles. "You're such a dreamer. Go, you silly."

"Oh. Right." Milla gets out of her mom's minivan. Then she leans over and pokes her head back in. "Mom?"

"Yeah, babe?"

"Do you ever . . ." She breaks off, unsure how to go on. *Do you ever not know who you are?* is part of it. Also, *Do you ever wish you were someone else?* But those are hard things to say out loud, especially when your mom seems so comfortable with herself. When both your moms seem totally comfortable with themselves.

Sometimes Milla feels different from the other girls at school because of having two moms.

Sometimes Milla feels different from her two moms because of being . . . well, just a plain old normal girl, the sort who would rather be the same as everyone else than different.

"Do I what, honey?" Mom Abigail asks.

Milla jumps. She forgot she'd asked a question.

"Um . . . do you think I look okay?" She smoothes her black yoga pants and stands up tall so that her white top hangs right.

"You look beautiful," Mom Abigail says. "You're a beautiful girl, inside and out."

Milla smiles unconvincingly, wishing it were true.

Nine

Violet

Violet hates this school. The hall is crowded and *everyone* is squealing. The squeals make her feel like a pinball being bounced back and forth.

Modessa! You highlighted your hair—it looks adorable!!!

Do I have food in my teeth? For real, do I?

Oh. My. God. Been to Salvation Army recently, Katie-Rose?

My guinea pig had babies!!!!!

Don't be mean. She has to wear it because of her religion.

Hold up! Wait for me!

Violet is bounced around by the squeals—pummeled,

really—but no bright lights flash and no prize bells go *ding ding ding!* Why? Because none of the squeals is directed at her. Because she is un-squeal-worthy. She's *the new girl,* and though she can feel people checking her out, not one person bothers to say "hello."

Everybody here is *so* snobby.

"Can you, um, tell me where Mr. Emerson's class is?" she asks a tiny Asian girl with pigtails. The last girl Violet asked ignored her. The last girl wore an insanely huge headgear, the newfangled kind that doesn't go around the wearer's head, but instead is held in place with a forehead brace and a chin brace. She looked like a medical experiment, that girl, but *still* she deemed Violet unworthy of a simple response.

Will this teeny pigtail girl in her bright yellow peasant blouse do the same?

"You're in Mr. Emerson's class?" the pigtail girl says. "Lucky!"

So Violet *is* visible. Her ribs open to let more air in. "Why?" she asks. "Is he nice?"

"Omigod, super nice. He's missing an arm, though— just so you know."

Violet blinks.

The pigtail girl waves it off like it's no big deal. "Car accident. Really sad. Just don't stare, and you'll be good." She sticks out her hand. "Hi, I'm Katie-Rose. I'm in Ms. Perez's class, blech. Not *blech* 'cause of Ms. Perez. She's actually super-nice, too. *Blech* because . . . *well . . ."*

Katie-Rose lets her sentence trickle off in a meaningful way, and Violet suspects she's supposed to say, "What? Tell me!"

But Violet is stuck on the arm thing, which *does* seem like a big deal. Katie-Rose might think it's not, but Katie-Rose still has two arms—one of which is hovering in front of Violet like a pale white fish. Violet shakes it, but as quickly as humanly possible. Since when do fifth graders shake hands?

"So . . . Mr. Emerson's room?" she repeats.

"That way," Katie-Rose says, gesturing exuberantly. She whacks a girl wearing a headscarf, who stumbles backward and crashes into a pretty blonde girl.

Both girls—headscarf girl and pretty blonde girl—go down. They go down *hard.*

It really is *a pinball game,* Violet thinks.

"Oh! I'm so sorry!" the headscarf girl cries from her sprawled position.

A third, beanpole-ish girl—still standing and not sprawled on the floor—glares at headscarf girl. Then she directs her attention to the pretty blonde girl. "Milla," she says, "are you okay?"

"I'm fine," the blonde girl says, looking dazed. Her backpack has spilled open. Her stuff is all over the floor. People step over it, or try to. Some pause briefly. Some laugh. Some scrunch their foreheads with concern, or with relief that it wasn't them.

"Nice, *Spaza*man," Beanpole says to the girl in the headscarf. "I see you didn't take coordination classes over the summer."

The girl in the headscarf blushes. Katie-Rose, Violet notices, seems to be inching away from the scene of the crime. She's certainly not waving her hand and saying, "No, really, it was me! My fault, so sorry!"

"Quin, hush," Milla says to Beanpole. She turns to the girl in the headscarf. "Yasaman, I'm fine."

Ahhhh, Violet thinks, matching names with faces.

Beanpole equals Quin, and the headscarf girl is Yasaman. Blonde falling girl equals Milla.

She goes over it again: Quin, Yasaman, Milla. And Katie-Rose, the teensy pigtail girl who's to blame for this collision. Only . . . where is she?

Violet glances around. Katie-Rose has dematerialized.

Yasaman gathers Milla's strewn belongings. Her eyes are so dark that Violet can't make out her pupils, and she's got the most amazing lashes Violet has ever seen. Thick, lush eyelashes that brush her brow bones when she glances at Milla.

"I . . . I don't know what happened," she explains. "I was just walking along, and . . . I think somebody bumped into me?"

"Yeah, uh-huh," Quin says. "What happened is that you're a *spaz*, Spazaman." She elbows Yasaman out of the way. "*I'll* help Milla get her things. You can go."

Quin shoves notebooks and glitter pens into Milla's backpack while Yasaman awkwardly gets to her feet. She wants to help Milla, Violet can tell. But Quin said *no*.

The bell rings, high and tinkly and not like Violet's old

school's bell at all, and the congestion in the hall clears. Soon the only people left are Milla, Quin, Violet, and Yasaman.

"Oh my God, *look*," Quin says, snatching and smoothing an escaped piece of paper. "Our logo—it could have gotten *crumpled!*" It doesn't look like anything special, just a printout of a panda bear with words underneath.

"But it didn't," Milla whispers. She seems embarrassed that Quin's making such a scene. "*Shhh.*"

As for Violet, she feels stupid and doesn't know why she's still standing there ... except she kinda wants to tell Yasaman it's okay?

Don't make friends with the class outcast, whispers a voice in Violet's brain. *You've got enough problems already, wouldn't you say?*

Yasaman hovers for another moment, then takes quick steps down the hall and disappears. Quin and Milla stand up. Quin swoops back down for one last item, a sparkly pink bracelet, and hands it to Milla.

"Geez, Milla, you carry around so much crap," Quin says, and Violet finds Quin's change in tone interesting.

With an audience, Quin was mean to Yasaman and sweet as pie to Milla. With her audience gone—all except for Violet—Quin no longer treats Milla like a precious doll.

"All this crap," Quin goes on, "and except for our logo, none of it's the slightest bit practical." She laughs. "If you got stranded on a mountain? You'd *totally* die."

"I have a Tootsie Pop," Milla says. Her eyes flit to Violet.

"A Tootsie Pop," Quin repeats. "Yay."

When Milla doesn't respond, Quin snaps her fingers in front of Milla's face.

"I'll see you at break," Quin says to Milla, and it's the spookiest thing how she honestly doesn't acknowledge Violet at all. "That's when we'll start recruiting."

Milla bites her lower lip, then nods. She goes one way, and Quin goes the other.

Now Violet's all by herself. Lovely. She'll be tardy on the first day and have to explain to her one-armed teacher why she couldn't be bothered to be on time.

She hitches her messenger bag higher on her shoulder, then pauses, spotting something small and bright. It's on the floor, by the wall. She walks over. She puts down her bag and squats.

Huh. It's a tiny wooden turtle, painted orange and red. It's cute. When Violet places it on her open palm, its head wobbles. She closes her fingers over it, and it grows still.

Ten

Katie-Rose

Katie-Rose feels terrible about the human domino effect in the hall. The human domino effect *she* triggered. For all she knows, she might have even pulled off the elusive reverse thingie Max has been preoccupied with. It wasn't pretty.

Thanks to Katie-Rose, Milla went down hard, the contents of her backpack skittering every which way. And then Yasaman ended up on the floor, too. And Quin was mean and called Yasaman names, and Katie-Rose dashed away like a chipmunk who was *this close* to being run over by a car.

Ag. Where is the Rewind button when Katie-Rose needs it?

FADE IN TO KATIE-ROSE'S FANTASY SEQUENCE:

INTERIOR RIVENDELL ELEMENTARY SCHOOL— HALLWAY—MORNING

The walls are plastered with colorful posters and artwork. PENNIES FOR PEACE! reads one hand-drawn sign. TEACHERS OPEN THE DOOR. IT'S UP TO YOU WHETHER YOU WALK THROUGH IT, reads another. Students head noisily to their classrooms.

By the water fountain, two girls pause. One girl is black and has a tense expression on her face. She's new. The other girl wears jeans and a yellow peasant blouse and looks like the type of person who would make an excellent friend. She would also make an excellent president of the United States one day, just for the record.

The new girl asks a question, and the girl in the peasant blouse happily stops and answers. In fact, she is EXCEEDINGLY WARM AND FRIENDLY ABOUT IT, even though the new girl doesn't give her much to work with in the way of smiling back.

> KATIE-ROSE
> (mid-sentence)
> —so just keep going straight and you'll see Mr. Emerson's room. And if you have any other questions, don't hesitate to ask, 'kay? Because I've been at Rivendell forever, and I pretty much know everything there is to know.

The new girl nods. She's really pretty, and she'd be even prettier if she didn't look so . . . detached.

> KATIE-ROSE (CONT'D)
> I can tell you about all the cliques and stuff, too. Like, there are certain girls who are nice and certain girls who are not, if you get my drift.

YASAMAN TERCAN approaches. Yasaman falls into the "nice girl" category, although she's kind of a fringe element as she doesn't hang with any certain group. Today she's wearing sneakers, jeans, and a long-sleeved shirt. Oh, and her hajib, of course. Last year Miss Akins made Yasaman give a presentation on what it meant to be Muslim, and everyone learned that the headscarves some Muslim women wear are called hajibs. Or, wait, maybe hijabs? Muslim girls don't usually wear them till they're older, but sometimes they do.

KATIE-ROSE

(to Yasaman)

Hi, Yasaman! It's so great to see you! How was your summer?

YASAMAN

Hi, Katie-Rose! It's great to see you, too!

Yasaman steps forward to hug Katie-Rose and accidentally hits an innocent passerby.

CAMERA PANS TO MILLA.

                    MILLA
                  (surprised)

    Oh no!

She stumbles, pinwheeling her arms. Yasaman's eyes
grow wide.

                 MILLA (CONT'D)
    I'm falling! Somebody help!

A really mean girl smiles cruelly. Her name is QUIN,
and she's shifty like a fox.

                    QUIN
                  (evilly)
    Ha ha ha ha ha! Seeing people fall is so funny!
    Ha ha ha ha ha!

CAMERA PANS TO KATIE-ROSE.

With characteristic quick-thinking-ness, Katie-Rose
leaps forward and grabs Milla's elbow.

KATIE-ROSE

~~Whoa there! Steady, girl!~~

(No, that's stupid. Milla's not a horse.)

TAKE TWO:

KATIE-ROSE

That was close. You okay?

MILLA

(gratefully)

Oh, Katie-Rose, thank you. I almost fell on my butt. If you hadn't been here, who knows what would have happened!

YASAMAN

(seeming dazed, as if she, too, has just escaped terrible humiliation)

Yes! Thank you, Katie-Rose! If not for your quick thinking . . .

Yasaman's words trickle off as the mean girl, Quin, roughly pushes her aside.

QUIN

(to Katie-Rose)

You ruined my fun! I like seeing people fall on their butts!

MILLA

Quin!

Katie-Rose puts her hands on her hips. Her eyes gleam.

KATIE-ROSE

Just like you like seeing people drink mud? Is that what you're saying?

MILLA

(gasping)

Katie-*Rose*!

Quin, the mean girl, takes a step back. She suddenly looks uncertain.

KATIE-ROSE

That's right, I know all about it. And I don't want it happening again, understand? No butt-falling, no mud-shakes. Got it?

Quin nods foolishly. ~~She had no idea Katie-Rose was so . . . . She never realized Katie-Rose was such a . . .~~ She trembles in the face of Katie-Rose's power, while Milla, Yasaman, and the new girl gaze at Katie-Rose with open admiration. The other kids in the hall applaud.

KATIE-ROSE

So let that be a lesson. You hear me, Quin?

THE IMAGE WAVERS.

KATIE-ROSE (CONT'D)

I said, do you—

DISSOLVE TO:

"—hear me, Katie-Rose?" Ms. Perez asks. Her smile is amused. "I've called your name three times."

Several kids laugh. Katie-Rose's face heats up.

"Sorry," she mumbles.

"It's okay, I know how hard it is coming back to school," Ms. Perez says.

"Especially for some of us," Quin says from her prized back-row seat. Ms. Perez doesn't hear her. Modessa does—and doesn't bother to smother her laugh.

"What I was saying is that I think Greek Week will be an excellent way to kick off our fifth-grade year," Ms. Perez says. "Mr. Emerson and I have come up with all sorts of activities: costumes, presentations, Potato Olympics—"

"Potato Olympics?" a guy named Chance says. "Sweet!"

Ms. Perez smiles. "And we've set it up to involve *lots* of class participation. I'll assign roles today, as well as research topics, and on Wednesday we'll get together with Mr. Emerson's class to share our findings. We'll all dress up as ancient Greeks, and each of you will report on a specific Greek character or myth."

"When do we do the Potato Olympics?" Chance asks. "Can we, like, make them do dogsled races?"

"Can we pick our own topics?" a guy named Preston asks.

"Sure, just run it by me first," Ms. Perez answers. She leans against the front of her desk. "You know what would be fun? We could decorate the commons with laurel leaves, and those of you who are artistic could make Greek theater masks in art class. We could even bring Greek snacks to munch on."

Her round face brightens at this idea. She scans the rows of students. "Do any of your mothers know how to make baklava?"

"No," Chance says.

"That'th thexthith," Natalia says.

"I'm sorry . . . what?" Ms. Perez says.

Natalia, the girl who loves Pokémon, has returned from summer break with headgear the size of a small planet. She lisps now, and perhaps this should give Katie-Rose perspective on the fact that everyone has problems, not just her. But it doesn't.

"*Thexthith*," Natalia says. "Why do you only care if our *momth* know how to make baklava? Couldn't our *dadth* make baklava, too?"

"Absolutely!" Ms. Perez beams. "Does your dad know how to make baklava, Natalia?"

"No, he never doth any of the cooking."

Modessa shoots her hand up. "I don't like baklava. Doesn't it have *paste* in it?"

Kids titter.

"Almond paste, Modessa," Ms. Perez says. "It's delicious."

"I don't like almonds," Modessa says. "Anyway, with all this Greek Week stuff"—she says "Greek Week" as if it's of very dubious benefit—"what's going to happen to the ice cream social?"

Chattering breaks out, a sudden flood of concern. The ice cream social is a tradition at Rivendell. It's on the first Friday of the year, and the parent volunteers go all out in terms of flavors and syrups and practically every sort of topping you could imagine.

"You can't cancel the ice cream social!" a girl named Ava says. "*Please*, Ms. Perez!"

Ms. Perez holds out her hands. "Class. Hush. No one's canceling the ice cream social."

"Thank *God*," Ava says, as others clap and hoot. Katie-Rose peeks over her shoulder to see Modessa sitting primly, as if she's personally responsible for restoring the hopes of the fifth grade.

"I'll speak slowly so that everyone understands," Ms. Perez says with a smile. "All week long, we'll be studying ancient Greece. On Wednesday, we'll dress up and give reports. Thursday is Potato Olympics. And that leaves Friday completely free and open for our ice cream social. Now, I know it's *complicated*, but I think it'll all work out."

Ms. Perez is teasing her class for getting so worked up, but not in a mean way. Even so, it puts Modessa in her place.

Katie-Rose decides she likes Ms. Perez.

"We're packing a lot into our first week, I know," Ms. Perez says. "That's why I want to go ahead and assign roles. Remember, this is just who you dress up as, not necessarily what you give your presentation on. So what do you say, Katie-Rose?"

Huh? Katie-Rose thinks. Then she remembers that *before* the baklava and *before* the ice cream social, there was a chunk of class when she had spaced out. And apparently during that chunk, Ms. Perez had asked her a question. What that question *was*, Katie-Rose has no idea.

"Um, yes?" she finally says.

"Terrific!" Ms. Perez exclaims.

"Oh my *God*," Quin says. Even without turning around, Katie-Rose knows Quin's snotty voice. "Talk about typecasting."

"I know, it's hilarious," Modessa says. Katie-Rose knows Modessa's voice, too—the lazy, liquid quality of it, like dishwashing soap.

"So on Wednesday, you'll come to school dressed as a servant girl from ancient Greece," Ms. Perez says.

"I will?" Katie-Rose blurts.

"And if we end up with some baklava, you can pass it out. Won't that be fun?"

No! Katie-Rose thinks. *Not fun at all!* Of all the possibilities, she got the role of *servant*?

"Thervant girlth mainly went around naked," Natalia says. "I know becauth of Altered Beath for Wii? The upgraded edition? You have to rethcue the goddeth Athena, and the thervant girlth are naked."

"Yes, thanks, Natalia," Ms. Perez says lightly as

everyone laughs and Katie-Rose tries to sink into the ground. "But don't worry, Katie-Rose. We won't subject you to that."

"You mean subject *us* to that," Modessa says.

Ms. Perez moves on. "We'll need some members of the upper class as well, so raise your hand if you'd like to be an Athenian citizen of status."

Hands shoot up, a rustling of hungry birds.

Ms. Perez selects a handful of students, and yes, Modessa and Quin's names are called. They are officially recognized as privileged members of the highest caste in school, and now Katie-Rose is no longer sure she's a fan of Ms. Perez after all. Does she have no memory of what it was like to be in fifth grade? How can she think it's a good idea to take two MEAN GIRLS who already think they're God's gift to the world and say, "Hey! You two! You're God's gift to the world!" Or ancient Greece's gift to the world, same difference.

And she, Katie-Rose, "volunteered" to be a servant. *Great. That's just great.*

She props her forehead against her fists and makes a personal, private *aaargh* sound. Only, did she accidentally say it out loud? Because someone is staring at her from the other side of the room. She can feel it. Not Quin and not Modessa. They're behind her, probably writing notes about how fabulous they are and how much of a joke Katie-Rose is.

She glances to her left, and her stomach plummets, because the staring person is Yasaman Tercan, the girl who took the blame when Milla tripped. The girl Katie-Rose *let* take the blame. She's watching Katie-Rose with dark, unreadable eyes.

Eleven

Yasaman

At 10:15, the fifth graders take their first break. That's the way it works at Rivendell. Then, at 11:30, they'll have lunch, followed by a second break. Lunch and both breaks take place outside on the playground, as long as the weather allows.

So, at 10:14, Ms. Perez says, "Okay, kids, go off and be free." Her classroom has a back door that opens onto the playground, and as soon as the words leave her lips, there's a loud, crazy exodus and much scraping of chairs on the floor.

Yasaman knows what to expect next. Outside, some

of the guys will play football, some basketball, some soccer. Some of the girls will play with them. That slightly odd boy, Max, will circle the playground endlessly with his best friend, Thomas, and they'll pretend to be Pokémon trainers. That's what they did last year, anyway.

Other things Yasaman knows from five years of watching her Rivendell classmates:

- Max and Katie-Rose are friends, but they don't hang out at school.
- Katie-Rose doesn't have many (or possibly *any*) other friends, especially not ones who are girls.
- Katie-Rose wants to have friends, though.
- What Katie-Rose really wants is to be BFFs with Milla Swanson, but Milla is part of the popular group, so it's unlikely to happen.
- The popular group is made up of Modessa (queen), Quin (second in command), and Camilla (third in command). Sometimes Modessa and Quin gang up on Milla, and when that happens, Milla sometimes ditches them, but only for a day. She always goes back.
- Once, last spring, Yasaman saw Milla staring at

herself in the mirror in the girls' bathroom. Not like *I'm so beautiful*, though she is. More like, *Who am I? Who is this person staring back at me?* Then Milla noticed Yasaman, and her expression reverted to perky and sweet (and, underneath, embarrassed).

Yasaman notices other things, too. Unimportant but interesting things, like how Carmen Glover picks her nose when no one's watching, but says, "I would *never* pick my nose. I used to, but I don't anymore." How the teachers have an unofficial "time-out" bench for when a kid breaks a rule and needs to be alone for a while. How Cyril Remkiwicz writes things down in a black spiral notebook but never ever shows it to anyone. It's some sort of scorecard, Yasaman thinks. Cyril will peer at someone and then scrawl down a number. Once Yasaman tried to get a better look, and he rotated violently away from her and hunched over his notebook to hide it.

Now, Yasaman is the last person to leave Ms. Perez's room. As she walks slowly onto the playground, her autopilot thought is, *Here we go again. Another year of sitting. Another year of watching.*

Unless . . .

A new thought slips into Yasaman's brain: *Unless you choose not to sit and watch. You could do that, you know. You could walk over to Katie-Rose and ask her what she was daydreaming about while Ms. Perez explained the ancient Greece unit.*

Whatever her daydream involved, Katie-Rose was so absorbed that Ms. Perez had to call her name three times when she was assigning the "You will be this person from ancient Greece" roles.

Yasaman is intrigued by how inwardly focused Katie-Rose was, because not everybody has that capacity. Mr. Aslan does; Yasaman saw it during her summer computer class. Her mom does; Yasaman sees it in the way she worries her lower lip while painting one of her tiny, painstakingly detailed pictures of flowers.

But her little sister, Nigar, for example, doesn't get intense about things. Nigar is cheerful nearly all the time and skips around and hums. She pretends their cat, Blackberry, is her baby, and she lugs him around and rocks him and puts hair bows in his fur. There's nothing Nigar gets *passionate* about, though.

Wouldn't it be cool if Katie-Rose had a secret passion? And . . . what if her secret passion was computers?

It probably isn't, Yasaman warns herself. *Don't get your hopes up.*

Still, her feet lead her to Katie-Rose. Anxiety squeezes her throat, but she keeps going.

Five feet away now.

Four.

Three.

She's two feet away when Katie-Rose spots her, but Katie-Rose doesn't respond the way Yasaman hoped. In fact, Katie-Rose steps back. *Quickly.*

Omigosh, she doesn't even want to talk to me, Yasaman thinks. Her fluttering heart says, *Run! Leave this big mistake NOW!*

She's about to do just that when she notices something probably no one else would. Katie-Rose is blinking. Like, a lot. *Blink, blink, blink.* And people don't blink when they're repulsed. They blink when they're nervous.

Katie-Rose—*omigosh, it's true*—is nervous.

Seeing that flips a switch in Yasaman, and *bam!*

Yasaman herself isn't nervous anymore. Instead, she wants to make Katie-Rose feel better.

"Hi," Yasaman says.

"*I-didn't-mean-to-I'm-so-sorry,*" Katie-Rose says in one big rush.

Yasaman wrinkles her forehead. "Excuse me?"

Katie-Rose blinks. "You know. About . . ."

"About what?"

Katie-Rose looks pained, and also a little annoyed, as if she doesn't want to explain it, whatever it is.

Ohhh, Yasaman thinks. Katie-Rose must have been there this morning when Yasaman bumped into Milla. Katie-Rose must have heard Quin call her "*Spaz*aman," and she feels bad in that way people do when they witness someone else's shame.

Yasaman doesn't want to go there, however. So she crosses her eyes and shrugs to say, *Yeah, not fun, but what can you do? Quin's stupid, anyway.*

Katie-Rose seems surprised. She blinks *again*, then offers a hesitant smile. Yasaman smiles back.

"So, I wanted to ask you something," Yasaman says.

"Ok-a-ay," Katie-Rose says.

"When Ms. Perez was explaining our ancient Greece unit . . . what were you thinking about?"

"What do you mean?" Katie-Rose asks suspiciously.

"You were in your own little world, that's all."

Katie-Rose hitches her shoulders. Her glance strays to the grassy area of the playground, where Quin, Modessa, and Milla are in a huddle.

Yasaman waits. Sometimes waiting is the best thing to do, and plus, she's had lots of practice.

"I was just thinking . . ."

Yasaman raises her eyebrows.

"Well, just about . . . you know. How in movies the good guy always wins."

"Oh?"

"See, I want to be a cinematographer when I grow up," Katie-Rose continues. Her eyes brighten, and her words spill out faster. "Or maybe a producer. I haven't decided for sure. But one or the other, and probably a screenwriter, too, so I can produce my own material."

Yasaman grins. Katie-Rose *does* have a passion—and even though it's not computers, it's still pretty cool.

"That's awesome," she says.

"I know," Katie-Rose replies, and Yasaman laughs.

"I mean, thanks," Katie-Rose says, turning pink. "I think it is, too. I've been filming stuff all summer—"

"You have a video camera?"

"Of course. Then I download my footage to iMovie and edit it. That's the *really* fun part. When I'm old enough, I'll probably post my movies on YouTube, which is a site on the internet where you can upload your own videos."

Katie-Rose pauses, her gaze drifting up to Yasaman's *hijab.* "Do you, um, know about the internet, Yasaman?"

"Katie-Rose, please," Yasaman says. "Just because I'm Muslim doesn't mean I live in the Dark Ages."

Katie-Rose's blush deepens. "Oh."

Yasaman's not mad, but she *is* enjoying Katie-Rose's discomfort. Or maybe she's just enjoying Katie-Rose, period. Talking to her and laughing and not being alone.

"Anyway," she says, "I was in Mrs. Gratz's computer class with you last year."

Katie-Rose's expression is classic *oops.* She could have a speech bubble over her head, that's how clear the *oops* is. Then she rearranges her features and attempts to recover her bravado.

"Well, have you heard of YouTube?" she asks. "Do you know what it means to upload videos and stuff?"

Yasaman smiles, wondering how Katie-Rose will respond when Yasaman tells her that not only does she know about uploading videos, but that she's created her own internet network, where someone—Katie-Rose, for example—wouldn't *have* to be a certain age in order to post her movies.

"What?" Katie-Rose demands. "Why are you smiling like that?"

Yasaman links her arm through Katie-Rose's—it's odd how natural it feels—and guides her to the vacant time-out bench. "Sit," she says. "I have *so* much to tell you."

Twelve

Camilla

Milla wants morning break to be over. She doesn't like the way Modessa and Quin have to pick apart every single girl in their grade, snidely detailing why not a single one of them is Panda material. Making fun of Katie-Rose's peasant blouse (which Milla happens to think is cute), mocking Natalia's new headgear, snickering—always snickering—about how clumsy Yasaman is and how stupid she looks with her head covered like an old lady's.

"But she has to wear it," Milla hears herself say. "It's for her religion."

Quin and Modessa look at her. Then they look at each other.

"*Camilla*," Modessa says, and her intonation is all that's needed to shut Milla up. Modessa shuts Quin up sometimes, too, but not as often, because Quin is a mini-Modessa. She agrees with everything Modessa says, and she knows what Modessa's going to say before she even says it, since in most cases Modessa's already texted Quin whatever it is.

Modessa and Quin *love* texting.

Milla probably would, too, if she had a cell phone. Though she would try hard not to text mean things.

Cell phones aren't technically allowed at Rivendell, but both Modessa and Quin have one anyway. Modessa's is sleek and black; Quin's is plain silver but with a leopard-print cover. Both girls *looooove* their cellies, but Quin's love comes awfully close to obsession. Maybe 'cause it's her lifeline to Modessa?

"There is *one* girl with potential," Modessa says. She jerks her chin at a girl from Milla's class. The new girl.

"She stared at me during morning announcements," Milla murmurs.

"Why, because you're so beautiful?" Modessa says, and it's somehow meant to put Milla down. Milla doesn't have a clue why the new girl was staring at her, only that she was.

"I like her style," Modessa pronounces, surveying the new girl's high boots and crisp gray skirt, which she's paired with a tailored green blouse. "Plus, she's fresh meat. She's got to be more interesting than the rest of these wannabes." She turns to Milla. "Milla, go get her."

"Wh-what?" Milla says.

It takes Quin a beat to catch up. Then she puffs her chest and says, "You heard her. Go *get* her."

Milla has a familiar feeling of *How did this happen? How did I get here?* Because what is she supposed to say? *Come here, new girl? Modessa wants you?*

She passes Katie-Rose as she approaches the swing set, and Katie-Rose calls out and waves. Katie-Rose is sitting with Yasaman Tercan, and if Milla weren't so distracted, she might stop to wonder why. Katie-Rose and Yasaman aren't friends, are they?

"Hi," Milla says vaguely.

She reaches the swing set and kind of edges in front

of the new girl, only not too in-your-face-ish. She feels bad for not knowing the new girl's name, but it's not her fault. The new girl got to class late. She checked in privately with Mr. Emerson at his desk.

"Um . . . hi," Milla says.

The new girl is startled. "What do you want?" she asks, jamming her hands behind her back.

Wow, Milla thinks. *Defensive much?*

But it's got to be hard, being the new kid in a school where pretty much everyone's known each other since pre-K.

Be nice, Milla tells herself.

"Well, I was, um, wondering . . ." She squinches one eye, a nervous habit she doesn't know she has. "See my friends over there?" She indicates Modessa and Quin. "They want to meet you."

"Why?" the new girl wants to know.

Milla shrugs.

The new girl sizes her up. Her hands circle around from behind her and dive deep into her front pockets.

"No, thanks."

Milla's eyebrows shoot up. *No, thanks?*

But they're Modessa and Quin, she wants to say. *You don't say "No, thanks" to Modessa and Quin. You say "yes, ma'am!" And maybe even salute.*

"Why not?" Milla asks.

"Why do you care?" the new girl shoots back.

"They—*we*—just want to meet you. We're in this club, kind of, and maybe you'll want to join."

"A club?"

"If they—*ack*. If *we* say it's okay, that is. If you pass all the tests." Gosh, she sounds ridiculous. *If you pass the tests?*

Milla glances over her shoulder at Modessa and Quin, who look impatient. She turns back to the new girl.

"We'll do tons of fun stuff, like hold bake sales, maybe. Or Pennies for Peace. We could help with that." She's winging it, as not one of these activities has actually been mentioned by Modessa or Quin. "And, um, we'll donate everything we earn to pandas."

"You can't donate Pennies for Peace to pandas," the new girl points out.

You can't? Milla thinks. And then she answers her own question: *Oh. Duh. Otherwise it would be Pennies for Pandas.*

But every so often, Milla surprises herself with her ability to think on her feet. "Well . . . if the pandas were fighting, you could."

The new girl's expression hardly changes. *Something happens, though. Something in her eyes, a sparkle, like one worthy opponent stepping up to another.*

"Hmm," she says, straight-faced. "There *is* a big problem with nonpeaceful pandas, I hear."

"In . . . Borneo," Milla contributes. *Does Borneo even have pandas? Where is Borneo? Is it possible Milla made Borneo up?*

"Right, the Great Borneo Panda War," the new girl says. "They keep stealing each other's bamboo."

"And poking each other with it."

"*Pandas,*" the new girl says in the resigned tone one might use when shaking one's head at a pack of boys making farting noises.

Milla suspects the new girl is suppressing a smile. She knows that she herself is.

"Quin made us a logo," she says. "I'll show you." She squats and unzips her backpack, hunting for the picture Quin downloaded of a panda with big eyes. Underneath,

Quin added the club's motto: ONLY THE BEST, FORGET THE REST.

Milla roots through her notebooks, her folders, a jumble of glitter pens. Where *is* that darn logo? Quin gave it back to her after she tripped and spilled the contents of her backpack . . . didn't she? Not being able to find it sends darts of panic up Milla's spine, because Milla needs everything to be *just so*.

She dedicates herself to a thorough inventory:

Seashell necklace: yes.

Keychain with the picture of her moms on it: yes.

Her cherry Tootsie Pop, a travel pack of Kleenex, a heart-shaped stone that Milla likes to rub. It's gold with glittery flecks and looks magical. And oh, good, there's the Panda picture, stuck in between the pages of her purple spiral.

But . . . where's Tally? *Where's Tally the Turtle???*

"Um, don't worry about it," the new girl says, sounding uncomfortable. "The logo, or whatever."

Milla glances at her, but doesn't really see her. Nor does it register that she's been squatting for a while, head practically swallowed by her backpack. She dives back in, because she can't stop now. Mom Joyce and Mom Abigail brought Tally to her from Guatemala, and Tally has even more magical powers than her heart stone, because of being *folk art* made by an actual shaman, which is like a lady witch, but a nice one.

"I have to worry about it," Milla says urgently. "She's my good-*luck* charm."

The new girl inches backward. "She?"

Omigosh, omigosh, omigosh, Milla thinks. Tally isn't in her backpack. She's searched every inch of it, and *Tally isn't there.*

She lifts her head and sees her fear mirrored in the new girl's face.

"My turtle," Milla wails. "I can't find Tally the Turtle!"

TUESDAY, AUGUST 25

Thirteen

Katie-Rose

L ife is lovely, and Katie-Rose is blooming with joy as she gets ready for her second day of fifth grade. *La la la*, she made a friend! A friend who likes computers and websites and HTML code! A friend who knows how to embed videos within blog sites!!!! Could life get any better?

She hums as she pulls on cropped jeans and a T-shirt that says GEEK MAGNET in a font that's supposed to look like ancient Greek letters. It's dorky, but appropriate, given the unit on ancient Greece the fifth graders are doing. *Yasaman will appreciate it,* she thinks. *And who cares if I have to be a servant tomorrow. Servant girls are cool. Way better to dress up as a servant girl with a fellow servant girl buddy than to be some hoity-toity Athenian citizen.*

Yep, Yasaman is a servant girl, too. Yesterday, during class, Katie-Rose was too wrapped up in her own thoughts to note who the other servants were. But last night, she and Yasaman chatted up a storm: about school, about Greek Week, about how if Ms. Perez were smarter, she would have assigned Modessa the Gorgon-she-monster role of Medusa, *heh heh heh.*

Medusa *is* from Greek mythology, after all. Yasaman Googled her as she and Katie-Rose chatted, and she reported that Medusa was said to be "made of terror," a description equally fitting for Modessa.

Then Katie-Rose did some Googling of her own and suggested that Quin was Modessa's harpy, "a snatcher of people and souls." *Hahahaha*, so perfect.

How did Katie-Rose and Yasaman do all of this chatting, while simultaneously Googling fiendish Greek beasties? By IMing on the site Yasaman created, Blah-BlahSomethingSomething.com! AND IT WAS AWESOME-TATIOUSFUL!

Seriously awesometatiousful. It wasn't all that different from IMing on AOL, only it *was*, because *Yasaman made the site herself.* Katie-Rose couldn't get over that. If Yasaman could build a website, was there any reason Katie-Rose couldn't *for real* film and produce a movie? No, there was not.

It's all about dreaming big, Yasaman had typed. It gave Katie-Rose the chills, because, okay, IMing was already cool, but IMing with Yasaman on an invisible, private site that only Yasaman knew about—and now Katie-Rose— well, there just weren't words to describe it.

Except awesometatiousful. *Seriously* awesometatiousful.

After exhausting the subject of Gorgons and harpies, Yasaman and Katie-Rose had moved on to more pleasant topics. For example, Yasaman told Katie-Rose all about Facebook and how she wanted to make her site be like that, only she wouldn't have a rule about having to be thirteen. Her only rule would be niceness. She told Katie-Rose about virtual cupcakes, too, and Katie-Rose typed, ????

they're like smilies, kinda, except they're cupcakes, Yasaman explained. sooooo cute!

She told Katie-Rose how her cousin sent virtual cup-cakes to her Facebook buddies, as well as virtual plants and virtual Starbucks drinks and even virtual name-brand purses.

Virtual *purses*? Katie-Rose responded. Lame. i bet u cld come up with better things to send than *purses*.

like what? Yasaman wanted to know.

I dunno, Katie-Rose typed. Like . . . like . . . virtual cheese puffs!

Then there was a pause, which made Katie-Rose nervous even though she knew by then that Yasaman was slower at typing than she was. Maybe Yasaman didn't like cheese puffs and Katie-Rose had offended her? But how could anyone not like cheese puffs? Anyway, were cheese puffs any reason to get mad at someone?

No. No, they weren't, and surely Yasaman wasn't.

(Wasn't *mad*, that is, not a cheese puff. Not that Yasaman was a *cheese puff*, either . . .)

At any rate, when Yasaman's response finally flashed onto Katie-Rose's screen, Katie-Rose felt a glorious lightness in her chest.

WE cld come up with better things, Yasaman's message said. U and me, and for sure we'll include virtual cheese puffs. and maybe 1 day we'll invite other girls to join 2? do u think?

Sure! Katie-Rose typed. Her smile stretched out her cheeks. I know *exactly* who we shld invite. camilla swanson!!!

That set off a whole flurry of messages, because although Yasaman liked Milla—she came right out and said so—she didn't think Milla would want to be a member of BlahBlahSomethingSomething.com. Katie-Rose won her over, of course. She got Yasaman to agree that they'd find Milla the very next day and ask her . . . unless for some reason they changed their minds. Which they wouldn't, because wasn't it Yasaman herself who said she wanted to invite other girls to join?

Katie-Rose could have chatted all night, but Yasaman had to log off to put her little sister to bed. *Boooo.*

Now, with the morning sun casting a pink glow on her bedroom walls, Katie-Rose snaps elastics around her pigtails and wonders if there's time to IM Yasaman right this very second, before school.

She *really* wants to.

Is this what druggies feel like? Or cigarette smokers who can't shake the habit? She giggles, imagining herself in a Computer Users Anonymous meeting. "Hi, my name is Katie-Rose, and I'm addicted to IMing," she'd say. "And now, good-bye. My screen name is The*rose*knows if you ever want to chat!"

From her desk, her laptop beckons. *Come to me!* it croons. *Wake me up and open your internet browser! Just a simple click of a button . . .*

Oh, what the heck, Katie-Rose thinks. Charlie and Sam are no doubt downstairs hogging the last of the Cap'n Crunch, and she'll get stuck with boring Product 19. But too bad. A need like hers cannot be denied.

She logs on to BlahBlahSomethingSomething.com with eager, trip-along fingers, praying Yasaman will be online. But she's not. No friendly avatar blinks on the side of the page to announce that Yasaman wants to chat.

Katie-Rose drums her fingers on the part of her laptop below the keyboard. She telepathically wills Yasaman to get her booty in the chat room.

Yasaman's booty is apparently otherwise engaged.

"Grrrrr," Katie-Rose says. She gets up, leaves her room, and grabs the upstairs phone from its base.

"Katie-Rose, is that you clomping around?" her mom calls. "Come eat your breakfast, bunny!"

"In a sec!" Katie-Rose calls back. She punches in Max's number. *Answer*, she coaches. *Answer, you big slowhead!*

"Hello?" Max says when he *finally* picks up.

"Hi, Max," Katie-Rose says. There's no need to introduce herself. "IM me, 'kay?"

"Um . . . my mom made pancakes," Max says.

"So? Bring your laptop to the table."

"I'm not allowed. Anyway, it would get sticky."

Katie-Rose groans. *Boys.*

"What do you need to tell me?" Max asks.

"Nothing," Katie-Rose says, slightly offended. Why would she *need* to tell him anything?

"So . . . why'd you call me?"

This is so *not going anywhere*, Katie-Rose thinks.

"Katie-Rose!" her mom calls. "Oatmeal gets gluey when it gets cold—you know that!"

Oatmeal? Blech. Even worse than Product 19.

"Bye, Max," she says.

"Bye, Katie-Rose. I finally mastered the elusive reverse domino effect, by the way. I can pretty much guarantee it to work every time now."

"Um . . . yay?" Katie-Rose says. She wants to feel glad for Max, but talking about dominoes makes her think of the Yasaman-Milla tripping incident, which makes her fingers tighten on the phone.

Then she remembers, *Wait! You're friends now, you and Yasaman. The tripping incident? Regrettable, but a thing of the past!*

This realization makes it so much easier to be happy for Max that she says, "How'd you do it?"

He goes into a long, detailed, Max-style explanation, which she tunes out. But when he ends with "So will you?" she *doesn't* say, "Of course, dearest Max!" The servant girl thing with Ms. Perez taught her better than that.

"Will I what?" she says.

"*Film* it for me," Max says. He pauses. "Were you even listening?"

"Well . . . no. Film what?"

"My five-hundred-domino course, complete with direction changers, a zipline, and at least one use of the elusive reverse domino effect."

"You made that? Holy cannoli!"

"Katie-*Rose*!" her mom calls. "Off the phone!"

"I haven't made it *yet*," Max says, a tad impatiently. "I'm still setting it up. I want you to film it once it's done."

"*Ohhhh. Of course*, dearest Max!"

The sound that comes out of him is mostly a laugh, though there's a cautious element mixed in. "Dearest Max" is not how Katie-Rose typically addresses him.

"Uh, great," he says. "This is my most ambitious project yet. I really want it to work."

"I'm sure it will," Katie-Rose says. "Oh, and just so you know, I'm friends with Yasaman now."

"Yasaman Tercan? Cool."

"I know," Katie-Rose says. She hangs up the phone, wishing she were at Rivendell with Yasaman already. This makes her realize something, and she mentally whacks herself. All morning, when she thought she was craving a jolt of instant messaging . . . well, she wasn't.

The buzzing Katie-Rose feels? It's a seed, that last

night turned into a sprout, that with every passing second is growing and stretching—only not toward a cold computer screen, but toward warmth and light. Toward Yasaman. Her friend.

She bolts downstairs, eager to choke down her gluey oatmeal and get to school.

Fourteen

Violet

Violet tugs open Rivendell's heavy front door
at the start of this new day and feels the gloom of
despair. *One day down, five million more to go.* And yet
she has no choice but to trudge through this day, and the
next day, and the next and the next and the next, so far
into infinity that Violet might as well curl up like a roly-
poly and give up now.

Only, if she curls up like a roly-poly in the middle of
this crowded elementary school, the principal will surely
cart her off to the loony bin.

Oh, well, she thinks fatalistically. *Bound to happen sooner or later.*

If Violet's mom were here, Violet could talk to her about how awful it is to be the new girl who doesn't know the ins and outs of the social food chain, which means not yet knowing who she's supposed to be friends with and who not. (Though she's starting to figure it out. It's kind of horrifyingly easy.)

If Violet's mom were here, Violet could talk to her about whether it even makes sense to worry about who to be friends with and who not. Maybe her mom would say, "Oh, Boo, you can't worry about what anyone else thinks. Who do *you* want to be friends with?"

And if Violet's mom were here, maybe she could help Violet figure out the whole Tally the Turtle mess. Like, why didn't Violet return that turtle she found to Milla yesterday? She didn't initially know *for sure* that the turtle belonged to Milla, but she had a pretty strong feeling. And later, out on the playground . . . why in the world didn't Violet make things right *then?*

"My turtle, my turtle!" Milla had wailed. *And Violet. Just. Stood there.* Seriously, what was that all about???

Violet doesn't *want* the stupid turtle. It's not that. She thinks—*maybe*—that it has to do with . . . oh, it sounds so petty and awful. With holding someone's happiness in the palm of her hand?

Now you have it, now you don't.

If Violet's mom were here, Violet wouldn't need to play God like that . . . *because she'd have her mom.*

If, if, if.

Violet's getting a headache. Kids push past her, and a sharp elbow knocks her ribcage. *Ouch.*

"Hey, new girl," someone calls.

The little hairs on the back of Violet's neck stand at attention. Slowly, she turns around.

"Give me a hand, will you?" It's Modessa, the girl Milla wanted to introduce Violet to yesterday . . . until Milla realized her turtle was missing and forgot Violet entirely in her crescendo of panic.

Violet has an inkling—*fine*, more than an inkling— that Modessa is Rivendell's Queen Bee.

Modessa smiles at Violet.

Violet approaches, careful not to show anything on her face.

Modessa's wearing a flippy black dress with criss-cross straps in the back, and her white-blonde hair is swept up into a sleek back-of-the-head bun. Her shoes are white ballet flats with black polka dots.

"I forgot your name," Modessa says, rolling her eyes as if she's a dunce. But it's an act, because Modessa never knew Violet's name in the first place, and Modessa doesn't for a moment think she's a dunce. Violet sees all that and more behind Modessa's smooth exterior.

Violet hesitates, then says, "V."

"V?" Modessa says. "Just V?"

Violet meets Modessa's gaze straight on. It's strange. With people like that Katie-Rose girl in the hall yesterday, and on the playground with Milla, Violet feels awkward and unsure of herself. But with someone like Modessa, who has power and flaunts it, Violet finds herself standing tall and throwing back her shoulders.

"Just V," Violet states. *You have a problem with that? Take it up with my therapist.*

"Hmm," Modessa says noncommittally. "Well, *V*, help me put this poster up."

Violet glances at the piece of poster board Modessa

is holding. It says, HELP FIND TALLY THE TURTLE! And under that, REWARD. CONTACT MODESSA, QUIN, OR MILLA WITH **ANY** INFORMATION.

Violet swallows as she takes the poster and holds it up to the wall. But her tone comes out casual when she asks, "Who's Tally the Turtle?"

Modessa puts her hands over Violet's and scooches the poster to the right to cover up a PENNIES FOR PEACE poster. She pulls a strip of tape from her roll. "Only my best friend's prized possession." She presses the tape over the poster's top corner. "She's *so* attached to it. She's probably got an attachment disorder or something, but whatever. I love her anyway."

The fact that Modessa insults Milla while at the same time claiming her doesn't escape Violet's notice.

"Is it a real turtle?" Violet asks. Tally's bobble-headed self stays mute in the side pocket of Violet's backpack, but Violet can feel its burning presence.

"It's a toy," Modessa says. "It probably cost all of fifty cents." She tapes up the other corner and flashes Violet a just-between-us smile that means, *Pretty dumb, I know.*

Violet returns the smile, thinking, *If Milla's your friend and you love her so much, you shouldn't make fun of her behind her back. Even if you do it trickily.*

"There," Modessa says, sticking on the last bit of tape. "Perfect."

"Hmm," Violet says noncommittally. It's a flawless imitation of Modessa, and she does it right in front of Modessa's model-perfect face.

Modessa's eyes widen, then narrow with displeasure. Then, deliberately, she smiles. "So keep a lookout, 'kay? And, hey—"

Here it comes, Violet thinks.

"You should sit with us at lunch. Me and Milla and Quin."

Violet knows what she's expected to say. She even knows *how* to say it—meaning, not too eager, because girls like Modessa don't like eager. So she gives Modessa what Modessa wants, all the while knowing that girls like Modessa don't like girls like Violet, either. Not deep down.

"Maybe," Violet says. She glances at her forearm and brushes off an imaginary bit of dirt.

"*Riiight*," Modessa says, as if she sees through Violet's ruse but respects her for it nonetheless. Her lips twitch. She grabs her messenger bag from the floor and spins on her heel. "See ya."

Violet watches Modessa stroll down the hall, noting how kids make a path for her. She's the Queen Bee, all right.

But Violet's no dummy. If Modessa were to look over her shoulder and *catch* Violet watching . . . well, whatever respect Modessa may have granted her would vanish immediately and without explanation.

Violet heads for Mr. Emerson's class. As she walks, she takes stock of her emotions, the way Dr. Altebrando taught her.

Is she happy?

No, happiness is out of Violet's reach.

Is she sad?

No. Why would she be sad when the most popular girl in the fifth grade just asked her to sit with her at lunch?

(Except . . . yes, maybe a little sad. Maybe a lot sad.)

Why?

Why not? LIFE is sad. Not being sad, that *would be worth noting.*

Violet straightens her spine, but keeps her limbs loose. She *strolls*, like Modessa.

Her headache is worse than before.

Fifteen

On the playground during morning break, Milla twines her new scarf through her fingers. It's lime green and sparkly, with a smattering of pink flowers on the ends, and until yesterday, it belonged to Mom Abigail. Milla has always loved it, and she knows that's why her mom gave it to her, as a replacement for Tally until Tally is found.

But Tally *hasn't* been found, and Milla saw the look Mom Abby exchanged with Mom Joyce. Her moms think Tally might not be found, ever.

Milla rubs one of the flowers between her thumb and forefinger as Modessa and Quin put the new girl, V, through her paces. Milla made an effort to catch the new girl's full name when Mr. Emerson called roll today, but the guys behind her were being loud. It might have been Vivian, or Viola, but it doesn't matter. The new girl prefers to go by V, so V it is.

Also? For the record? V didn't give Milla the time of day during their morning spelling lesson *or* their class discussion of Greek gods and goddesses. She acted as if yesterday's playground weirdness never happened.

"V, go find out what color Ms. Perez's underwear is," Modessa commands.

V arches her eyebrows. "Excuse me?"

"Go find out what color Ms. Perez's *underwear* is," Modessa repeats, fake patiently.

"No, thanks. I don't even know who Ms. Perez *is.*" V replicates Modessa's tone exactly, and Milla gives her points for ballsiness. She's a rare match for Modessa.

"Me and Modessa's teacher?" Quin says, like *duh.*

"We're, like, doing the ancient Greece unit with your class?"

"She's over by the swing set," Modessa says. She gives a head-jerk. "El Fatty over there who eats too much baklava."

Milla is embarrassed. Ms. Perez is on the largish side, and in her thirties at least, and wears clothes that are too young for her, like Juicy track pants and T-shirts from Victoria's Secret. From the Pink line. Modessa seems to have something against her, but Milla thinks she's nice—and she loves the butterscotch highlights in her glossy dark hair.

The ball's back in V's court, and Milla watches V's emotions play over her face. First, *That's so dumb.* Then, *But, fine. You think I won't, so I will.*

"*Eeeee!*" Quin squeals as V strides toward the swing set. "Oh my God, she's doing it!" She uses her leopard-skinned celly to snap a picture.

"Of course she is," Modessa replies. But she's pleased, too. "I think we should give her probationary Club Panda status—*if* she comes back with the answer." She turns to Milla. "Milla, do you agree?"

Milla doesn't respond.

"Ca*milla*," Modessa says. She huffs. "You're worrying about your stupid turtle again, aren't you?"

Milla draws back. She *is* worried about Tally. It's true. (Though Tally isn't stupid.) But why would Modessa be mad at her for that?

"We put up *all* those posters and we went to *every single classroom* to make announcements," Modessa says. "We've done everything that can be done."

Milla rubs the pink flower on her scarf. The pink, plus the sparkly green of the scarf, are the only splotches of color in her otherwise all-white outfit. Maybe that's why Modessa's mad?

"*Camilla!*" Modessa says impatiently.

"What?" Milla says. *I'm looking at you,* she thinks. *I'm listening. What have I done wrong this time?*

"There *are* other things in life besides your problems," Modessa says.

"Yeah," Quin contributes. She aims her cell phone at Milla and takes *her* picture.

Milla flinches at the metallic *beep*. Then her attention is pulled away by an unexpected sight. Is that . . . is that Katie-Rose heading in her direction? With Yasaman Tercan?!

"I just think you need to get your *priorities* in order," Modessa says.

"Yeah," says Quin.

"Like, you could totally make more of an effort with V," Modessa continues. "She's the one who helped with the Find Tally posters. Just FYI."

Maybe Katie-Rose and Yasaman really are *friends,* Milla thinks. *But why are they coming over here? Katie-Rose knows how Quin and Modessa feel about her.*

Apparently, Katie-Rose doesn't care. She and Yasaman are chatty and bubbly as they approach, and it's Yasaman who seems to falter when she catches Milla's expression. She stops in her tracks, and Katie-Rose has to tug on her to start her up again.

From the other side of the playground, Milla sees V start back toward them. V is approaching from a different angle than Katie-Rose and Yasaman, but they're all three heading toward the same destination.

Oh gosh, they're going to meet in the middle, Milla realizes. *And . . . cripes. I'm the middle.*

"You haven't even thanked her," Quin accuses.

Milla jumps. "Huh?"

"For the *posters*."

"Oh. Right!" She meets Modessa's stare. "Thank you. Thank you *so* much."

"Not me," Modessa says. "*V.*" She juts her chin. "Here she comes. Milla, ask what she found out about Ms. Perez's underwear."

"But I don't—"

V is upon them. "Red," she reports without prompting. "And it's a *thong*."

"*Ewww!*" Quin says delightedly.

Katie-Rose and Yasaman have reached Modessa's posse, too, though they're a few feet back. So far no one's noticed them but Milla.

"Milla," Katie-Rose says in a *really* loud whisper. "Come here."

Milla pretends not to hear. Katie-Rose's shirt says GEEK MAGNET, and Milla can only imagine the field day Modessa would have with that.

"How did you find out?" Modessa asks V. "Visible butt crack?"

Please don't talk about Ms. Perez's butt crack, Milla thinks. It's wrong and disrespectful and just . . . *wrong*.

Quin snickers. "I should have given you my phone, V. Then you could have taken a picture of it." Snicker, snicker. "Of Ms. Perez's *visible butt crack*."

Katie-Rose's head swivels to Quin.

Uh-oh, Milla thinks.

"Why are you being mean to Ms. Perez?" Katie-Rose asks.

Milla steps between them. Maybe if Katie-Rose can't see Quin, she'll let it go. And maybe if Quin doesn't see Katie-Rose, she won't . . . well, do whatever obnoxious anti-Katie-Rose thing she decides to do.

To her credit, V blushes. "I didn't see any VBC." She steals a glance at Katie-Rose. "I only saw . . . you know."

"Her *thong*," Quin says in a singsong voice. "Ms. Perez wears a tho-ong. Ms. Perez wears a tho-ong."

Milla wishes Quin would shut up—or that she was brave enough to tell her to shut up.

Milla feels an elbow in her side. It's Katie-Rose, butting into the inner circle.

"That is *so* inappropriate," she says to Quin, planting

her hands on her hips. She turns to include Modessa. "You shouldn't talk about teachers' . . . *bottoms.*"

Quin and Modessa are speechless—and then they burst into laughter. Like, roll-on-the-floor laughter, only they aren't rolling, because they're on the playground and they'd get dirty.

"Omigod," Modessa says, gasping. "Quin, we shouldn't talk about teachers' bottoms."

Milla's stomach tightens. When V calls Modessa on her crap, it earns Modessa's respect, but when Katie-Rose does the same thing, Modessa laughs as if Katie-Rose is nothing but a worthless speck. *Why?*

Some deep part of Milla senses the answer, and it's such an ugly truth about human nature that she is shot through with shame.

"Katie-Rose is right," she whispers to Quin and Modessa. "You shouldn't."

Modessa's eyes pop. Still laughing, she says, "What is this, the Anti-Being-Mean-to-Bottoms League?"

"Yes," Katie-Rose shoots back.

Modessa's laughter trickles off, and Milla thinks, *Uh-oh.* Because Modessa, as Milla knows, gets more pleasure from certain other things than she does from laughter.

Run, Katie-Rose, Milla begs her silently.

But Katie-Rose doesn't, and Modessa gives her a slow, thorough once-over. "'Geek magnet'?" she says, reading Katie-Rose's shirt. "Oh, sweetie, I don't think so. You're not going to attract anyone, ever, not even a geek."

Katie-Rose turns a bright, painful red, and Milla hurts for her, because she knows—she *knows*—what it's like to be on the receiving end of Modessa's assaults.

Snicker snicker snicker, goes Quin.

"I want to talk to Milla," Katie-Rose says stiffly. She turns away from Modessa and looks at Milla, who drops her gaze to her sneakers. They're solid white Skechers, but there's a smudge on her left toe. She'll have to wash them tonight.

"What do you want to talk to her about?" Quin asks. "Her *bottom*?"

"Come on, Katie-Rose," Milla hears Yasaman say. "Just forget it."

"I don't want to forget it," Katie-Rose says.

"Sure you do," Modessa says easily. Pleasantly, even.

Modessa can go from mean to nice so quickly that it scares Milla. It's like with Modessa, *anything* can happen.

"Milla?" Katie-Rose says with a slight tremble.

Milla closes her eyes. *Go away, go away, go away*, she thinks. *Everybody just GO AWAY.*

"She's not going to answer you," Modessa tells Katie-Rose.

"Shut up, *Medusa*," Katie-Rose says.

Milla's eyes snap open. *Medusa*. Katie-Rose just called Modessa *Medusa*. Milla's vision goes preternaturally sharp, and she can see every individual thread woven in the fabric of her smudged white Skecher.

Elsewhere on the playground, people are still playing. But not here. Here, everyone waits—in horror, in delight—for Modessa to turn Katie-Rose to stone.

"Oh, Katie-*Rose*," Modessa says, and it's dreadful, the feigned sadness at what a *disappointment* Katie-Rose is.

"I didn't mean to call you that," Katie-Rose says, low, quick, and—*oh, but it's too late*—scared. Milla can hear the fear fluttering in her voice.

"You hurt my feelings," Modessa chides.

"Yeah, you hurt her feelings," Quin says.

V opens her mouth like maybe she wants to interrupt, maybe even on Katie-Rose's behalf. Then she presses her lips together. To Milla's new eyes, V looks too sharp, just like her Skechers. Milla sees more than she wants to, which is that V isn't as ballsy as she lets on. Not when it matters.

"Come on," Yasaman says to Katie-Rose. "Let's go."

Milla decides to shut her eyes again. She doesn't open them until she's sure Yasaman and Katie-Rose have disappeared.

Sixteen

Yasaman

Yasaman:	hi, katie-rose! i'm soooo glad yr online!
The*rose*knows:	grrrrrr
Yasaman:	oh no. r u still upset about what happened on the playground?
The*rose*knows:	milla's not always like that, i swear. over the summer, she was . . .
Yasaman:	i know
The*rose*knows:	no u don't. u don't even know what i was going to say.
The*rose*knows:	i was *going* to say, if u hadn't

	interrupted me, that in pioneer camp, milla was . . .
Yasaman:	i didn't *interrupt* u. u stopped typing and did dot-dot-dots, and then u did it AGAIN. dot-dot-dots mean i'm allowed to jump in.
The*rose*knows:	oh. well, i like dot-dot-dots
Yasaman:	i'm worried about u, k-r. not just cuz of milla. cuz of . . . u know
The*rose*knows:	medusa. yeah, whatever. i'm a goner. if rivendell had lockers, i'd be stuffed in 1 right now.
Yasaman:	not right NOW. it's after school hours.
Yasaman:	2morrow, maybe . . .
The*rose*knows:	+looks at yasaman grimly+ gee. thx.
Yasaman:	do u think u shld . . . apologize?
The*rose*knows:	to MEDUSA??? no, never, and no again. If she beats me up, she beats me up.
Yasaman:	oh, k-r, i don't think she's going to *beat u up.*
The*rose*knows:	i know. +sighs+
Yasaman:	i think she'll do something worse
The*rose*knows:	?!?!?!?!?!!!!! Yasaman!!!!

Yasaman:	i'm sorry. like I said, i'm worried about u
The*rose*knows:	well, there's nothing i can do about it except stay out of her way. which i gladly will . . . even tho we're in the same class and ms. perez is making us do all sorts of stupid "sharing" with our greek research.
The*rose*knows:	think i shld share our "made of terror" theory?
Yasaman:	um . . . no. but speaking of that, i do have something to cheer u up.
The*rose*knows:	yeah?
Yasaman:	for the greek myth u pick to tell everyone about? u shld do how the rose was created!!!
The*rose*knows:	there's a myth about that? how *was* the rose created?
Yasaman:	well, one day a goddess was taking a walk in the woods, and she found the lifeless body of a nymph.
The*rose*knows:	oh joy. i'm not so excited about how this is starting, Yasaman.
Yasaman:	just wait. the goddess turned the nymph

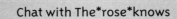

into a flower, and then she got her other god and goddess buddies to give her two gifts: beauty and a lovely odor

The*rose*knows: hee hee, i have a lovely odor

Yasaman: and that is how the rose was created and rightfully crowned "Queen of Flowers"!

The*rose*knows: huh. i like that. only, the rose is a *nice* queen, right?

Yasaman: yes, a very nice queen. or maybe she decided to just be a rose, and not worry about the queen part, and just soak up the sunshine and enjoy her lovely odor.

The*rose*knows: aw, that's sweet

The*rose*knows: thx, yasaman

Yasaman: yr welcome

Yasaman: so . . . do u still want to talk about milla?

The*rose*knows: not really

The*rose*knows: i mean, yes

The*rose*knows: and what i was gonna say, when we first started chatting, was that . . . well . . .

Yasaman: milla was different at pioneer camp. right?

The*rose*knows: how'd u know?

Yasaman:	ppl do that. they act different around different ppl.
The*rose*knows:	*i* don't
Yasaman:	actually . . . u kinda do
The*rose*knows:	no i don't!
Yasaman:	well, u acted different toward ME
Yasaman:	before this year, that is
The*rose*knows:	nuh-uh
The*rose*knows:	i did?
Yasaman:	+waits silently while katie-rose figures it out+
The*rose*knows:	HOW?
Yasaman:	+says *la la la* a couple jillion times as an avoidance technique+
Yasaman:	i stole yr +writing out stage directions+ thing, btw. do u mind?
The*rose*knows:	+puts hands on hips and huffs+
Yasaman:	+arches eyebrows+
The*rose*knows:	+rolls eyes+ cld we focus here, plz?
The*rose*knows:	uh what were we talking about?
Yasaman:	how u treated me different last year. do u really need me to explain?

The*rose*knows: well, u & i didn't *hang out*, if that's what u mean. but that was just cuz i didn't *know* u.

Yasaman: it was more than that

Yasaman: u hardly ever made eye contact. u NEVER said, "hey, wanna eat lunch with me?" u pretty much assumed i was just THAT WEIRD MUSLIM GIRL.

Yasaman: am i right?

The*rose*knows: um. um.

Yasaman: everybody treats me that way, not just u. don't worry

Yasaman: i'm just saying that milla being friends with u in pioneer camp doesn't equal milla being friends with u at school.

The*rose*knows: but WHY????

Yasaman: cuz the milla u hung out with over the summer . . . well, u got to know her all by herself. in a prairie outfit. but she's not that milla anymore. now she's back to being milla-who-hangs-with-modessa-and-quin.

The*rose*knows: i still don't understand WHY?!!!

Yasaman: we all have our roles. she's milla the popular

	girl, i'm that weird muslim girl, and ur . . . somewhere in between.
The*rose*knows:	but that's ridiculous
Yasaman:	yep
The*rose*knows:	today on the playground, she wouldn't even talk to me. she just kept staring at her feet.
Yasaman:	yep
The*rose*knows:	+sighs+
The*rose*knows:	i might have to dot-dot-dot for a while, cuz my brain . . . i dunno . . .
Yasaman:	u can dot-dot-dot as much as u need.
The*rose*knows:	thx
The*rose*knows:	er, yasaman?
Yasaman:	hmm?
The*rose*knows:	i like IMing with u
Yasaman:	i'm glad. me 2.
The*rose*knows:	and i'm sorry i . . . u know. ignored u last year.
Yasaman:	+smiles in a kinda embarrassed way, but happy, too+
Yasaman:	thanks. and i forgive u. +smiles some more+

The*rose*knows: so . . . do u, like, pray to allah and stuff?

Yasaman: "allah and stuff." my dad would flip

The*rose*knows: oh no, was that bad? i didn't mean anything bad. did i offend u???

Yasaman: it's just the whole "different" thing again

Yasaman: but yes, i pray to Allah. u can ask me other questions if u want.

The*rose*knows: ok, maybe

The*rose*knows: but for now i'd rather think about how we're ALIKE instead of how we're DIFFERENT—and that goes for milla, 2. i'm gonna make her c that i'm the same katie-rose from pioneer camp, and that things don't have to be different just cuz we're back at school.

Yasaman: r u sure? what if u make modessa mad again?

The*rose*knows: i know. i'll get milla to go to the computer lab with me before we do our myth presentations, and i'll show her blahblahsomethingsomething.com, cuz i know she'll luv it.

The*rose*knows: we've GOT to come up with a better name, tho

Yasaman: i wanna add smilies, 2. i'm gonna work on that tonite after i finish my report.

The*rose*knows: we have so much homework now that we're in 5th grade!!!! tonite i have to do my report *and* put my costume together, and then as soon as all that's over, BANG! we've got to start working on potato olympics

Yasaman: it's fun, tho

The*rose*knows: except for being servant girls. +makes face+

The*rose*knows: hey, i know. maybe . . .

ThePlaceForCollPeople?

Yasaman: huh? what r coll people?

The*rose*knows: no, i meant COOL ppl! The Place for Cool People—that's what we cld name our site. whaddaya think?

Yasaman: uh, no

Yasaman: but keep trying!!!!

Seventeen

Violet

Violet is exhausted, but she can't fall asleep. She tries regulating her breathing like her therapist taught her. Breathe in, two, three, four; out, two, three, four. She gets light-headed, but her thoughts continue to zip about every which way, refusing to be tamed.

Next, she imagines a ball of light hovering over her breastbone, radiating peace and serenity. Only, it's a really scrawny ball. A stupid ball. It shrivels and dies.

She flips to her other side and executes an aggressive sheet-adjusting maneuver, kicking to free the fabric caught beneath her hip. When did she get so angry? Has she always been so angry? It's like her body is filled with putrid green bile, and *everything* makes her mad.

(stop it, you're being a brat.)

So?

(so, this isn't you. you've got to stop . . . being so clenched up.)

Pfff. Yeah, right. Thanks for the brilliant tip.

(it's not Mom's fault that she . . .)

Yes it is. Shut up.

There's a rap on her door.

"Violet?" her dad says.

Violet freezes. She quick-pretends to be asleep.

There's a sliver of silence, followed by a creak as he opens her door. Stupid falling-down house, not nearly as nice as the one they left behind.

"You're rattling the floorboards, Boo," her dad says, and the nickname brings a rush of longing to her chest. A longing for the way things used to be, before her mom turned into a spook and her life turned into a ghost story.

Her dad comes to her bed. He hesitates, then sits on

the edge of the mattress. His weight is solid and shifts her universe. Still, she keeps her eyes shut.

He puts his hand on her back, traces rough circles. He never was good at back rubs. "If you're worried about your mother—"

"*I'm not*," she says fiercely, then curses herself for blowing her cover. She sighs and rolls over, looking up at him.

His eyes, when they connect with hers, fill with tears. But there's strength in his gaze, too.

"We're going to be okay, Violet," he tells her.

She aches to believe him.

"I spoke with Dr. Banks. He said she's responding well to the new medication, though it makes her thirsty. He's working on adjusting the dosage."

"Whoop-de-do," Violet whispers, then regrets it immediately.

Her dad takes her hand in his, and he doesn't go away, even though she's giving him very little to work with.

"We can visit her this weekend if you'd like," her dad says.

A lump forms in Violet's throat. "Whatever."

He nods, slowly. "Get some sleep, Boo," he says, leaning over and kissing her cheek. "Have fun tomorrow during Greek Day."

She exhales.

"Do you . . . feel like you're settling in? Now that it's been a couple of days?"

"Not really. Maybe."

"Want to tell me about it?"

She *could*, she supposes. Not about Modessa and Milla and . . .

(the turtle you stole.)

Not about any of that. But she could tell him about the Greek god, Hermes, whom she's presenting on tomorrow in front of both fifth-grade classes. She could tell him about how Mr. Emerson let her be an Athenian lady of stature, which means she has to wear a *chitōn*, which is the fancy word for toga. Which she doesn't know how to make, though she figures it's just a sheet tied in a fancy toga way.

She could . . . she could even ask him for help, maybe. With the sheet. He'd look stern and say, "Violet, isn't it a little late to be telling me about this?" But he'd figure something out, because he's good at stuff like that.

And while they worked on her *chitōn*, she could tell him that she thinks the concept of Potato Olympics is actually pretty clever, and that that's happening on Thursday if he wants to come watch, and that she's going to make her potato do the high dive into a bucket of water. She could tell him she no longer thinks Rivendell is *quite* as stupid as she first did.

She could tell him all that stuff . . . and deep inside she wants to. But as she gathers her courage, he makes a sound of resignation.

"Well, all right," he says, standing up from her bed. "Good night, Violet." He walks with weary footsteps across her room and leaves, shutting the door behind him.

And here you are, she tells herself, heavy with despair. *This is your life now.*

Her gaze drifts over her room. *Those Pottery Barn Kids pink curtains left behind by the previous owners? Yours. The garage-sale dresser with knobs instead of handles? Yours. The bobble-head turtle on top of the dresser?*

(NOT yours and you KNOW it. why haven't you given it back?)

The lump in Violet's throat won't go away . . . and what

is it, that lump? What physical reality is in there, lodged like a golf ball and pushing against the soft tissue of her throat? At what point did Violet's emotions get so bottled up inside of her that they took on a shape of their own?

Modessa and Quin and Milla—Violet knows they aren't nice girls.

(Well, Milla *might* not be so bad. Milla isn't the one who came up with the underwear dare and thought it was oh-so-hilarious that chubby Ms. Perez wore a thong. That was Modessa. And Milla didn't make fun of the Muslim girl who rammed into her and sent her sprawling. That was Quin. And while Milla didn't stand up for Katie-Rose on the playground—Katie-Rose, who shook Violet's hand on the first day of school—she wasn't out-and-out mean to her, either. That was Modessa *and* Quin.)

Here's something else that Violet knows, however. With Modessa and Quin, what she sees is what she gets. Modessa and Quin are pretty girls who wear the right clothes and have the right hair and know the right answer to the question of what's cool and what's not. After all, they're the ones asking the question.

Modessa and Quin assume that they're popular

because they're *meant* to be popular. They think they're getting what they deserve. Violet could tell them that that isn't the way it works, but why bother? Modessa and Quin aren't going to change. They're going to lord it over others their whole lives, and when they grow up, they'll drive their kids to school in skinny jeans and oversized Chanel sunglasses and make the dumpy, frizzy-haired, can't-quite-figure-out-what-day-it-is moms blink and say, "Oh *no*. I was supposed to bring brownies *today*?" and then burst into tears while everyone looks on.

So who cares about girls like Modessa and Quin?

Violet might *use* them, sure. Go along with their "tests." Lie about Ms. Perez's underwear. Let them think they're gracing her with their approval, when really she could care less.

It's easier to be one of the Populars, that's all. If you're a Popular, people don't mess with you.

But Milla . . .

That's where things get complicated, because fine, Violet knows perfectly well that Milla *is* different from Modessa and Quin. She can see the cracks in Milla's shell.

Violet thinks about the containers that filled the

cabinets of their old kitchen. Small cardboard boxes holding foil-backed sheets of pills, each pill safe within its hermetically sealed plastic pouch. Each pill trapped in its bubble of stale air.

Milla is not hermetically sealed. She may be a Popular on the outside, but on the inside, more tender things nudge against her. And this isn't good, this isn't good at all, because if Violet sees *Milla* struggling with doubts, then Violet might succumb to her own.

(stop. you're not like this. this isn't you!)

No, Violet has to stay strong. Strong like a goddess, lofty and untouchable.

And forget the chitōn. *If you're not mortal, why dress like one?*

(but . . . then . . . ?)

The ridiculous Greek-goddess outfit Aunt Sylvia brought her from Disneyland—Violet will wear that. It's from the movie *Hercules*, after all. And if Mr. Emerson doesn't like it? Too bad.

Her costume decided upon, Violet turns a cold eye to Tally the Turtle, sitting on Violet's dresser.

You're not giving that turtle back, you know.

(violet! no!)

Hey, Violet's mean voice says. *If Tally the Turtle means so much to Milla, then Milla should have taken better care of her.*

When you're careless with things you love, you don't deserve to keep them.

WEDNESDAY, AUGUST 26

❖ Eighteen ❖

Katie-Rose

(Shot from Katie-Rose's sunshine-yellow video camera)

FADE IN:

EXTERIOR KATIE-ROSE'S HOUSE—FRONT
PORCH—BEFORE SCHOOL ON WEDNESDAY
MORNING

                    KATIE-ROSE (off-screen)

Hi, Max!

Max, who has a red bedsheet wrapped lumpily around his body, glances over from the end of his driveway. He picks up the newspaper.

MAX

Hi, Katie-Rose. How are your social skills coming?

KATIE-ROSE (off-screen)

Ha ha. It was never *my* social skills that were in question.

Max ambles over to Katie-Rose's house and sits on the front porch. The image on the camera jiggles as Katie-Rose lowers herself down beside him.

MAX

But I thought . . .

KATIE-ROSE (off-screen)

You thought what?

MAX

Well, yesterday . . . and the playground . . . and
you were with Camilla, but—

KATIE-ROSE (off-screen)

(cutting him off)

Those were *her* social skills being a problem.
Anyway, doesn't matter. Yasaman explained
to me how people change depending on who
they're with, so today I'm going to get Milla by
herself. *Then* she'll be the real Milla.

MAX

Oh . . . . How do you know that the Milla with
you is the real Milla, and not the Milla with
Modessa and Quin?

KATIE-ROSE (off-screen)

Because when she's with Medusa and her evil
harpy, Quin, she turns into a shrunken, wimpy
version of herself, which is *not* the real her.

MAX

But even if she is the "real" her with you, what good does that do? Doesn't she always go running back to Modessa and Quin?

KATIE-ROSE (off-screen)

Do you have to be so negative? You can only say she *always* goes running back as long as the "always" is true. But once the "always" goes away, then it's not true anymore.

Max scratches his ear.

MAX

So ... what's up with the camera?

KATIE-ROSE (off-screen)

(proudly)

Ms. Perez said I could be the official documentariast of Greek Week. Documentarian?

(short pause)

Anyway, I get to documentize—*aaaargh*! I'm

going to film everyone's presentations. Isn't that awesome?

Max draws out a huge glob of earwax.

MAX

Check it out. *Sweet*.

KATIE-ROSE (off-screen)

Ewww! *Not* sweet! Disgusting!

Max extends his finger so that Katie-Rose can admire it.

MAX

On *MythBusters* once, they made a candle out of earwax.

CLOSE-UP ON GLOB OF EARWAX.

KATIE-ROSE (off-screen)

What's *MythBusters*'?

MAX

It's this show on the Discovery Channel. They do stuff like re-create the Hindenburg to see what went wrong, or they see if roach poison can set a house on fire. Stuff like that.

KATIE-ROSE (off-screen)

And they made a *candle* out of some guy's earwax?

MAX

They wanted to see which burned better: earwax or normal wax.

KATIE-ROSE (off-screen)

And?

MAX

The earwax. It burned forever. But apparently it was really stinky, so the MythBusters con-cluded that earwax candles wouldn't be a good product.

PULL BACK TO SHOW MAX'S FACE, RIGHT AS
HE'S SNIFFING HIS GLOB OF EARWAX.

                    MAX
    You know, if I accumulated enough ...

            KATIE-ROSE (off-screen)
    No. *Un*-awesometatiousful, Max.

                    MAX
    I could collect donations. I could start with all
    the earwax in our neighborhood, and then ask
    around at school—

            KATIE-ROSE (off-screen)
    Stop right there or I am going to throw up IN
    YOUR HAIR. Which needs brushing, by the
    way.

Max absent-mindedly rakes his fingers through his
bottle-brush hair.

MAX

Maybe I'll get one of those plastic gelato spoons—know the ones I'm talking about? Like miniature shovels?

KATIE-ROSE (off-screen)

NOOOOOO.

Max tries to look innocent, as if he has no clue why Katie-Rose is yelling at him. He can't quite hide his grin, though.

MAX

Hey, want to come see what I've got of my domino course so far? I mastered the elusive reverse domino, but now another problem's developed. Maybe you could take a look?

KATIE-ROSE (off-screen)

What good would I do? You're the domino genius.

From off-screen comes the sound of a door opening.

PAN TO FRONT DOOR.

Katie-Rose's mom pokes her head out of the house.

KATIE-ROSE'S MOM

Aren't you supposed to be in your Greek costume, bun-bun?

KATIE-ROSE (off-screen)

Wanna see Max's earwax?

From the far edge of the camera angle, Max can be seen offering it up obligingly. Katie-Rose's mother wrinkles her nose.

KATIE-ROSE'S MOM

Ew. *Max*.

KATIE-ROSE (off-screen)

He wants to make a candle out of it.

KATIE-ROSE'S MOM

Pretty small candle . . .

PAN TO MAX.

Max blushes. He leans over and wipes the glob of earwax on the leaves of a bush.

KATIE-ROSE'S MOM (off-screen)

Not on my lilacs!

Off-screen, Katie-Rose laughs.

KATIE-ROSE'S MOM (CONT'D)

And Katie-Rose, turn off your camera and come put on your servant girl outfit.

KATIE-ROSE (off-screen)

Fine, fine.

MAX

But what about my domino course? Because

mentally, I'm dealing with some fatigue issues, and it worries me.

The image on the camera jiggles as Katie-Rose stands.

KATIE-ROSE (off-screen)

I'm worried, too, Max. Believe me.

CAMERA SHUTS OFF.

FADE TO BLACK.

Camilla

Tally the Turtle still hasn't shown up, and Milla is heartbroken. She knows it's just a turtle . . . except at the same time, it's *not*. It's Tally. It's her good-luck charm. And if Milla's luck is so bad that she loses her good-luck charm, well, what's to stop the roof from flying off her house the next time a storm hits? Or both moms being in a car accident? Or everyone in her whole family dying, including her grandparents and uncles and aunts and cousins, even the ones from Texas she never sees? What if everyone in her family dies, plus every single friend, plus everyone she just plain knows?

If every single person she knew died, Milla would want to die, too. Not that she would commit suicide, because Mom Abigail had a college friend who committed suicide, and Mom Abigail said it was awful. She said her friend took a whole container of Advil and waited, alone, in her dorm room. Then—and this is the worst part—her stomach started cramping, and she got scared and called 911. An ambulance rushed her to the hospital, but it was too late.

That's the part that kills Milla. That Mom Abigail's friend *changed her mind.* That she got scared and changed her mind ... but too bad, there was no going back.

At her desk in Mr. Emerson's classroom, Milla gives herself a shake. Along with her pristine noblewoman's *chitōn*, which Mom Abby spent half of yesterday making from a pattern, she's wearing her lime green sparkly scarf for the second day in a row. She knows ancient Greek noblewomen didn't wear sparkly green scarves, but without Tally, she needs something to hold on to.

"Pssst," someone says. It's Katie-Rose, out in the hall. Beckoning. "*Psssst.*"

I have never actually heard someone say "pssst," Milla thinks. *Leave it to Katie-Rose.*

Milla feels bad about how she treated Katie-Rose yesterday on the playground, so she raises her hand and asks Mr. Emerson if she can go to the bathroom. As always, when Milla raises her hand in Mr. Emerson's class, she feels guilty, as if she's drawing attention to the fact that Mr. Emerson only has *one* hand to raise, should he want to. Milla knows she's being dumb—how many hands would he need to raise? nobody raises *both* their hands to ask to go to the bathroom—but that's how she feels.

"Yes, Camilla," Mr. Emerson says. "Come get the pass."

Milla scrambles out of her desk and goes up front, where Mr. Emerson keeps a kayak oar with the word GIRLS carved into the handle. He has another oar carved with the word BOYS. They're the biggest bathroom passes Milla has ever seen. She wonders where Mr. Emerson got them, and if he kayaks. Is it possible to kayak with only one arm?

Stop thinking about his arm, Milla tells herself. She prays that losing Tally the Turtle isn't a sign she's going to lose one of *her* arms.

Although I'd rather lose an arm than my entire family plus everyone I know . . .

"Milla!" Katie-Rose says as soon as Milla steps out of the room. "Come on—there's something I have to show you."

"Um, okay." She angles the kayak oar so that it doesn't bang against the walls.

Katie-Rose leads Milla to the computer lab and tells her to leave the oar outside. Milla obeys, which is kind of her way of saying "sorry" to Katie-Rose about yesterday.

"So . . . what do you want to show me?" she asks.

Katie-Rose glances at the back of the room, where the lab monitor is plugging numbers into a graph. She grabs Milla, guides her into a chair, and nudges the chair closer to a computer. Katie-Rose pulls up a second chair.

"Now," Katie-Rose says officiously. "We all know you like IMing, right?"

"Uh . . ." Milla glances at the lab monitor, wondering who "we" is.

"Just say yes," Katie-Rose commands. Her fingers fly over the keys. Katie-Rose is like the best typist in the whole fifth grade.

"Yes?" Milla says.

"Well, look!" Katie-Rose says proudly. On the screen appears a website called BlahBlahSomethingSomething. com. The words are bubble-shaped and orange. Glitter sparkles around each letter so they appear to be shimmering.

"BlahBlahSomethingSomething.com?" Milla says.

"And look *here*." Katie-Rose hits Return, and a members list pops up:

Yasaman

The*rose*knows

Milla's intrigued, but wary. If Modessa came in and saw her geeking out with Katie-Rose . . .

"Did you make this website?" she says.

Katie-Rose's fingers are at it again. "Are you kidding? I wish. No, Yasaman did—and she's really sweet and funny, and here's her blog, see?"

Milla peers at Yasaman's one entry:

Things about me:

I like frogs

I love books

I love movies, too, but I'm not allowed to see very many

Oh, and I LOVE orange and I LOVE school and I just know this is going to be the best year ever!!!

"She likes . . . frogs?" Milla says dubiously.

Katie-Rose shoots Milla a sharp look, and Milla shrinks. There's nothing wrong with frogs, she supposes. Just as there's nothing wrong with turtles.

"I like frogs, too," she amends.

"Well, excellent, because you can become a member!" Katie-Rose says. "And you can help us come up with a better name, because BlahBlahSomethingSomething.com is pretty lame, I admit. But isn't the site *totally* awesometatiousful?"

"What can you do besides IM and have a blog?" Milla says.

Katie-Rose pulls up a new page. "Tons of things. You can make your own profile. See? I haven't gotten to work on mine much, 'cause of all our Greek stuff—*groan*—but I picked out my wallpaper. The old-timey film projectors are 'cause I want to be a cinematographer one day. Yasaman's is polka-dotted."

Katie-Rose clicks, and Milla catches a glimpse of tangerine polka dots.

"Who knew, right?" Katie-Rose says. She clicks again, and a new screen appears. This page is called the Chatterbox! and on the right hand of the page is a rectangle full of emoticons, winking and waving and doing their things.

"Ooo, yay, Yasaman added smileys!" Katie-Rose says. "Let's try them out. We *have* to try them out."

Katie-Rose does some fancy tap-tap-tapping, and the page fills up with pigs:

"They are so cute!" Katie-Rose squeals. "Do you love them so much? Ooo, cupcakes, too! Yasaman said she wanted cupcakes!!!"

"This is making me hungry," Katie-Rose says when her finger stops punching keys. She regards Milla hopefully. "Do you think they'll have cupcakes in the commons, when we do our presentations?"

"Um, no," Milla says. "I think there'll be . . . figs. Or . . . Greek food."

"They *could* have cupcakes," Katie-Rose says.

"*Truuue*," Milla says carefully. They could also have

MoonPies and giant pink bunnies and free iPods for every kid in the school, but Milla knows they won't.

Katie-Rose snaps back into brisk, efficient Katie-Rose mode.

"So, yeah, this is the chat room, that's why it's called the Chatterbox. If there's more than two of us online, we can go there to talk instead of straight-up IMing. And we can share music, and make avatars, and eventually add applications like Make Your Own Button and stuff like that. It's going to be like Facebook, basically. Only better."

"And Yasaman made all this?" Milla asks. "*How*?"

"'Cause she's brilliant, that's how," Katie-Rose says. "Under that *hajib* of hers is one smart brain, and I should know." She waggles her eyebrows. "It takes one to know one."

Milla can't help but giggle. Katie-Rose is so full of herself—and yet, Milla suspects she doesn't *mean* to be obnoxious. And to her credit, Katie-Rose is equally generous in her assessment of others. Well, certain others. Like Yasaman, and how easily Katie-Rose said, "'Cause she's brilliant, that's how."

Milla cannot for the life of her imagine Modessa

saying something like that. Modessa's compliments fall more along the lines of, "Seriously, Milla, be *happy* you've got big feet. I would die to be able to borrow my mom's shoes."

This thought sobers her, and she says, "Actually, I think it's called a *hijab*."

"Huh?"

"*Hijab*, not *hajib*. The scarf Yasaman wears."

"I'd say it's more of a head covering," Katie-Rose says. "A 'scarf' is what *you're* wearing. It's totally different."

"Katie-Rose . . . do you realize you just corrected my correction?"

Katie-Rose wrinkles her brow. Then she laughs. "Oh my gosh, I did." She whacks her forehead. "I am such a dingleberry."

"Katie-*Rose!*" Milla exclaims.

"I am! I don't mean to be, but I am." She crosses her eyes. "Such. A. *Dingle*berry."

Milla's giggles are back, to the power of ten squillion. "Do you even know what a dingleberry is?!"

"Yeah! A stupid person."

"*No.* A dingleberry . . ."

She can't say it.

"What?" Katie-Rose demands. "A dingleberry is what?!"

Milla's laughing so hard she might pee. She's vaguely aware of the lab monitor's head jerking up, just as she's vaguely aware of someone—a girl, white-blonde hair— hovering outside the computer lab.

Milla tries to pull herself together, but *oh*, it feels good. All that laughter makes it easier to breathe.

She puts her mouth to Katie-Rose's ear and whispers, "A dingleberry is a teeny bit of poop that, um, stays stuck even after you wipe."

Katie-Rose's eyes bug out. She claps her hands over her mouth and leaps up out of her chair as if she can run away from the dreadful dingleberry.

"Ew! No! I take it back!" she squeals. "I am *not* a dingleberry!"

"*Girls!*" the lab monitor says in a shocked tone.

Red-faced and giggle-snorting, Milla says, "I've got to go, or Mr. Emerson's going to think I fell into the toilet."

"With the dingleberries," Katie-Rose manages. "Of which I am *not* one!"

Milla stands. She flips her scarf over her shoulder.

"Wait!" Katie-Rose says. "So will you join?"

"Huh?"

"You know. BlahBlahSomethingSomething.com."

"You guys have *got* to change the name."

"I know, I know. So will you?"

Milla hesitates. She should just say *sorry, I just can't*, because c'mon. Club Panda? Modessa's standards?

"I asked Yasaman to make you a button with Tally the Turtle on it," Katie-Rose says. "It's a virtual button, not a real button, but still." She navigates to a screen called Katie-Rose's Bling and pulls up a button icon that looks like this:

"Isn't it cute?" Katie-Rose says. "We want to make it say 'hi,' but we haven't figured out how."

Milla looks at the button icon and feels a swelling of . . . love? No, not love. That's too strong. But something like love, because Katie-Rose doesn't think Tally the Turtle is dumb. She doesn't think Milla should be "over it already." And Yasaman, based on her blog, seems nice, too.

"Okay, I'll join," Milla says, surprising herself.

Katie-Rose beams. Milla feels slightly sick at what she's just promised . . . but (maybe) slightly happy, too.

As she leaves the lab and grabs the kayak-oar bathroom pass, something catches her eye. She looks toward the movement just in time to see Modessa, garbed in a black tunic over black leggings, disappear around the corner.

Twenty

Yasaman

Yasaman's in the stall at the far end of the girls' bathroom. She's about to flush when she hears the bathroom door swing open. She hears two girls enter, and she freezes, because she recognizes one of their voices. *Modessa*, who's not on Yasaman's top five list of People She'd Like to End Up on a Deserted Island With. She's not even on her top five million, and not just because she was mean to Katie-Rose yesterday.

Last year, Yasaman and Modessa were in the same class, and during their unit on the Middle East, Modessa said, "That's where the ragheads live." Then she looked straight at Yasaman and said, "Oops. Sorry, *Spaz*aman."

Their teacher, Ms. Avery, forced both Modessa *and* Yasaman to stay in during afternoon break.

"We don't discriminate, and we don't use ethnic slurs," Ms. Avery told Modessa, who widened her eyes and said, "Oh my God, you are so right. I didn't even think!"

"Well, I want you two to engage in a *dialogue* about your differences," Ms. Avery said, closing the door behind her as she followed the rest of the class out to the playground.

"Thanks a lot," Modessa said to Yasaman.

"Excuse me? You're the hater who got us into this," Yasaman said. Only, she didn't say it out loud, because Modessa *was* a hater. A very powerful hater.

Modessa folded her arms over her chest. She stared at Yasaman, while Yasaman found her gaze shifting every which way.

Make recess end, she prayed. *Make recess end*.

"I heard about that Muslim dad, you know," Modessa said.

Yasaman felt a cold weight settle in her stomach. "I have no idea what you're talking about."

"How he killed his daughter?" Modessa said. "Right here in *America*?! All because she wore tight jeans. And then he buried her in his backyard, because she'd brought *shame* on his family."

Yasaman felt herself turn red, because she, too, had heard that particular story on the news. Bad Muslim father. *Horrible* Muslim father. But not all Muslims were like that.

"Is that why you wear those stupid baggy jeans?" Modessa asked. "So your dad doesn't strangle you and bury you in your backyard?"

"Yeah, that's why," Yasaman said, and this time the words *did* come out, because *come on*. She wanted to say something worse, but her *baba*'s teachings were ingrained firmly inside her. *Allah hates one who utters coarse language. The tongue that reads Quran should never be the same tongue that swears.*

The two of them spent the rest of break in silence. Modessa read a fashion magazine she wasn't supposed to have, and Yasaman tried to remember that Modessa didn't get to make her feel bad. She didn't have that power, even if it felt like she did.

When Ms. Avery finally set them free, they told her that, yes, their "dialogue" brought them one step closer to global peace and understanding.

Yet here in the bathroom a full year later, Yasaman has no desire to burst out of her stall and lavish hugs and air kisses on Modessa and whomever she's with. No, Yasaman's going to sit tight, thanks very much. And pull her feet up onto the toilet seat.

"What gets me—what *worries* me—is that she's just not making good decisions," Modessa says to mystery girl number two. "I mean, she was talking to *Katie-Rose*. She was *laughing* with Katie-Rose! The very day after Katie-Rose called me . . . what she called me!"

Yasaman goes cold. She *knew* Modessa would hold a grudge about that.

"It just shows poor judgment," Modessa says. "And plus, what's Milla going to do, lead Katie-Rose on and then dump her? That's just cruel. Right, V?"

V? Yasaman thinks.

She shifts to get a better angle through the crack in

the bathroom door, and yep, it's the new girl. The one Modessa and Quin were bossing around yesterday on the playground. She's wearing the coolest Greek goddess outfit ever: a gold-braided halter and a flounced skirt with more gold braid. But this isn't really the time to be noticing clothes.

From her slivered view, Yasaman watches Modessa finger-comb her shiny blonde hair. Modessa's wearing a black beaded tunic, but it's only marginally Greek-looking, and Yasaman hopes she gets in trouble. "How do you think I should pay Katie-Rose back?"

"What?" V says.

"For what she called me. What else?" Modessa pulls her cell phone from a hidden pocket in her tunic—she is *not* supposed to have her cell phone at school, and she's certainly not supposed to actually use it—and punches a button. Whatever she sees makes her snort. "*Quin.* Omigod, *so* needy."

V regards Modessa with disdain, which raises Yasaman's hopes. Maybe V hasn't been fully sucked into Modessa's web of evil? Although V masks her reaction the second Modessa puts away her cell phone.

"Let me see if I've got this straight," V says. "You want Milla to drop Katie-Rose because Katie-Rose called you 'Medusa'?"

Yasaman claps her hand over her mouth. She can't believe V just said that.

Modessa looks put out. In a *big* way. "Well, it's her decision, obviously." Modessa digs around in her messenger bag. "But who you hang out with in elementary school determines who you hang out with in middle school, right?" She slicks a layer of berry-colored gloss over her lips and gives three small smacks to even out the color. She holds out the tube to V. "Want some?"

Wordlessly, V puts some on. It looks better against her dark skin than against Modessa's light complexion, and a shadow crosses Modessa's face.

"Hmm," Modessa says. "Not your color." She grabs a scratchy paper towel from the dispenser and holds it out to V. Only, V doesn't take it. She looks at it, and then she looks at Modessa. *She doesn't take the paper towel.*

Omigosh, Yasaman thinks, thrilled. *Omigosh, omigosh!*

Modessa crumples the paper towel. "Fine, if you don't mind looking trashy."

V shrugs, and Yasaman mentally cheers. *Yes!*

"Anyway," Modessa says as twin spots of color form on her cheeks. "We need to get Camilla back on track. For her own good."

What you mean is that you need to get V back on track, Yasaman thinks. *V's not letting you have the upper hand, and you can't stand it.*

"And how do you plan to do that?" V asks.

"I don't know. That's why I'm asking you."

"You *are*?"

"Forget it," Modessa says. She pushes away from the sink. She's two feet from Yasaman's stall, and Yasaman really hopes she doesn't lose her balance and fall off the seat. Her quads quiver with the strain of holding still.

Modessa turns back to V. She can't let it go after all. "Maybe that dumb turtle."

V stiffens. "Milla's turtle? Did you . . . find it?"

"No," Modessa says impatiently. "And she's still all worried about it. I know she is. If I *did* find it, she'd pretty much kiss my feet."

There is wariness in V's eyes. "I just think she wants it back."

"Um, *yeah*. That's what I'm saying."

"So if you did find it . . . you'd give it to her?" Violet hesitates. "You wouldn't . . . do something mean?"

"Why would I do something mean?" Modessa says, and Yasaman's mouth opens, because it's as if Modessa believes what she's saying. That she *isn't* mean. That there's nothing wrong with wanting to find Milla's turtle not to make Milla happy, but to make Milla kiss her feet.

V breaks her eye contact with Modessa and fiddles with one of the bangles on her goddess outfit. "Well, if I wanted to find a toy turtle, I'd just look for it."

Modessa snorts. "You think, Sherlock?"

"We should go," V says. "We're supposed to be in the commons."

"Oh joy, *presentations*," Modessa says as both girls head for the door. Yasaman allows herself to collapse against the side of the stall.

"Maybe you'll get lucky. Maybe you can use the time to look for Milla's turtle," V says over the sound of bathroom door swinging open. "After all, isn't that what you want?"

Twenty-one

Violet

*T**here,* Violet *thinks* after wedging Tally the Turtle between the cushions of the beat-up sofa in the commons. The commons is the most central place at Rivendell, and it's where the two fifth-grade classes are getting together to do their presentations. Like, starting in two minutes. And so far every time the two fifth-grade classes have met—for group sing on Monday, for a lecture on library etiquette yesterday—the beat-up sofa is what Modessa has claimed for her throne. The other fifth graders don't even go near it, because it's got Modessa's scent all over it.

Modessa will sit there for our presentations, Violet thinks. *She'll find Tally and return her to Milla, and Milla won't be sad anymore, and no one will know I had anything to do with it. Everyone wins.*

Violet lifts her chin as she slips into the mass of costumed fifth graders entering the commons. Not in a snobby way, just a this-is-who-I-am way. She bumps into Katie-Rose, who's holding a video camera out in front of her and filming everything.

"Where did you come from?" Violet says.

Katie-Rose doesn't stop filming. "My mother's tummy. You?"

"Ha ha," Violet says uneasily. Did Katie-Rose see her with Tally the Turtle? *No, or she'd have said something,* she decides. Anyway, Katie-Rose is totally absorbed in her filming, moving her camera slowly to get a panoramic view of the room. She's different behind the lens—confident, but without her usual know-it-all-ness. *It's a good fit,* Violet thinks. It's as if . . . as if being behind the camera lets Katie-Rose be truer to who she really is, because it protects her from what scares her, kind of.

Everybody hides, Violet thinks. *Some in better ways than others.*

Violet swallows. *Moving on.* She angles past Katie-Rose and goes to the back of the commons. There are plates of pomegranates and baklava set up on a table, and Violet feels good enough to take some of each. Neatly folding in on herself, she takes a seat on the carpet.

Modessa, she thinks. *Where in the world are—?*

Ah. There she is, sauntering in with Quin. They're chatting and laughing and doing eye-roll-y things that mean, *Oh my God, check out so-and-so, I know.*

Just sit on the stupid sofa, Violet coaches them. She holds her breath.

They do, and when Modessa frowns, hikes up her bum, and fumbles to see what's poking her, sparks dance in Violet's brain. *Pop, pop, pop.* It's relief, mixed with lack of oxygen, and *pffooof.* Violet exhales and takes a big bite of baklava, shifting her gaze happily from the sofa just in time to see Milla standing above her.

"Good?" Milla asks.

"Huh?" Violet says. "*Oh*, the baklava. It's awesome."

She smiles at Milla—why not?—and scooches over, patting the floor to say, *Hey, sit here.*

Up front, Mr. Emerson says, "All right, kids, what do you say we start?" Ms. Perez is up there with him. Nobody's paying attention.

"Are you ready to give your presentation?" Violet asks Milla. There are fifth graders all around them. Everyone is squished, except of course Modessa and Quin. But who cares? Milla smells nice, like some sort of fruity shampoo, and Violet is airy with the knowledge of her good deed.

"Pretty much," Milla says hesitantly. She seems confused when Violet offers her a bloodred piece of pomegranate, but she accepts it.

"Who's it on?" Violet persists. *You don't have to worry anymore*, she wants to tell her. *Make your eyes stop doing that sad thing.*

"Um . . . I got assigned Apate," Milla says. "She was one of the evil spirits inside Pandora's box. She was full of"—she bites the end of her tongue and turns her glance upward—"deceit, guile, and trickery."

"Ooh, that's no good," Violet says.

"And one day Hera—Zeus's wife?—was mad at Zeus

because Zeus didn't want to, um, have any more babies with her."

"Really," Violet says.

"So she went looking for Apate, because Apate was known as the crafty one."

"Oh no, the crafty one!" Violet says in an on-purpose funny voice. Violet used to make funny voices all the time, but then she stopped. She's only doing it now to make Milla quit looking so worried.

Is this the first funny voice she's made since moving here?

Milla ducks her head so that her hair falls over half her face. "Hera wanted to borrow Apate's bewitching girdle."

"Her what?"

"Her bewitching girdle. That's what it said in my mythology book."

Violet peers at Milla. From behind her hair curtain, Milla peers back. They giggle at the same time, because "bewitching girdle" is even funnier than "the crafty one."

"Apate was bad news, though," Milla says. "She had lots of power, but it was bad power."

Hmm, Violet thinks. *Sounds like someone I know.* She strains her neck to see Modessa, because shouldn't she be returning Tally to Milla about now? Modessa *found* Tally. Violet saw her. So why isn't she presenting her to Milla in a flurry of . . . bewitching fakeness?

"All right, class. For real," Mr. Emerson says, ringing a cowbell. Everyone gradually grows quiet, and Violet thinks, *Oh well. Soon, though. She'll surely do it soon.*

"Who wants to go first?" Mr. Emerson asks.

"Wait!" a girl says. It's the girl with the ginormous headgear, who today is wearing some sort of very bizarre . . . horse-riding outfit? A Greek horse-riding outfit? She types frantically on her laptop, leaning sideways and scribbling into a notebook open on the floor.

"Natalia, you were supposed to get your homework done at home," Mr. Emerson says. "That's why it's called *home*work."

The fifth graders laugh.

"Thorry," Natalia says. "But I had thoccer last night, and then youth group, and I was *thoooooo* tired." She writes one last thing and slams shut her laptop with a flourish. "But it'th done, thee?"

"Why don't you go on and be first, then," Mr. Emerson says.

"Uh . . ."

"You *do* have your report? It's right there in your hands?"

"Uh . . ."

Violet looks at Milla. Natalia may have written her report, but it's clear she isn't prepared to actually give her presentation. She probably went straight to Wikipedia, looked up her god, and copied the entry word for word into her notebook.

"Go ahead, please," Mr. Emerson says. "We've got a lot of reports to get through."

He knows, too, Violet thinks.

Natalia walks reluctantly to the front of the class. She clears her throat. "Thatyrth were Greek godth with flat notheth, long curly hair, and goat hornth."

"Huh?" Violet whispers.

"I think she means *satyrs*," Milla says. "Those pointy-eared guys?"

"They love wine and women and every thort of phythical pleathure," Natalia continues with the single-mindedness of struggling with unfamiliar material.

Mr. Emerson frowns. "Natalia—"

"Their thpecial talent, which earned them honor and rethpect…"

Mr. Emerson hops up from his desk and fast-walks toward her.

" . . . wath their ability to balanth wine cupth on their…" Natalia frowns. "On their *erect*—"

"Okay, I think I'll stop you there," Mr. Emerson says.

Natalia's head snaps up. "It says their erect *penitheth*, Mr. Emerson!"

A ripple runs through the commons.

"Did she say what I think she said?" Violet asks Milla.

"Yet another reason to do your homework at home," Mr. Emerson says grimly, taking the paper from Natalia's hands. "Do you remember the part of the assignment that said *only share appropriate details?*"

"But *why?*" Natalia asks Mr. Emerson. "Why would they balanth wine glatheth on their—"

"Thank you, yes, and now you're done," Mr. Emerson says. *Everyone* is vibrating with glee, even Milla. Violet is glad to see her worry lines go away.

Mr. Emerson steers Natalia to her spot on the floor. "The Greeks were . . . an interesting bunch."

"That's for sure," Violet whispers to Milla.

Natalia resists Mr. Emerson. "But—"

"Story over. Ask your parents when you get home." Mr. Emerson frowns. "On second thought, don't. That goes for the rest of you rats, too—*if* you want me to keep my job, that is."

Everybody laughs. Mr. Emerson is so cool.

"Let's have someone else give their report," Ms. Perez jumps in. "Brannen? You have the Cyclops, right? Why don't you come tell everyone about the Cyclops."

As Brannen clumps forward to tell everyone about the Cyclops, Milla leans toward Violet. Her cheeks are rosy.

"Oh my gosh, I can't be*lieve* what a PG-13 day I've had," she says. She hesitates. "If I tell you something, will you promise to keep it to yourself?"

"Sure," Violet says, knowing she's good—sometimes too good—at keeping things to herself. But this is different. This is Milla *choosing* to share, and Violet is choosing to accept.

"You can't be mean to her about it," Milla warns. "You can't tease her."

"Tease who?"

"The person I'm going to tell you something about."

"Oh," Violet says. "I won't. I swear."

Milla pulls her knees up to hide behind. Violet follows suit, clamping her goddess skirt between her calves and thighs so she doesn't flash anyone.

"There's this girl," Milla says. "Her name's Katie-Rose—do you know who she is?"

Violet nods.

Milla lowers her voice to the barest whisper. "She called herself a *dingleberry*."

"What?!"

"She didn't *mean* to," Milla says. "She didn't even know what one was. Do you?"

Violet does, thanks to an abundance of male cousins. She makes a face, and Milla laughs in delight.

Violet likes making Milla laugh. She wants to do it again. She has a brainstorm and says innocently, "Apate must have had a dingleberry problem. Don't you think?"

"Huh?"

Violet pauses. She takes time to imagine Apate having some . . . hygiene challenges, the sort that would discourage potential suitors. "Why else would she . . . *you* know." She widens her eyes. "Need a bewitching girdle?"

"V!!!" Milla gasps. The laughter that bursts out of her is the best kind ever: fizzy like ginger ale.

Mr. Emerson's hand lands on Violet's shoulder. Both girls jump.

"Settle down," he says. "Cyclops isn't that funny."

"Yessir," Milla says. She waits until he's gone, then whispers, "Omigosh, V, I'm so sorry. I did *not* mean to get you in trouble."

"Milla," Violet says, "*I'm* the one who got us in trouble."

"Oh," Milla says. She processes. "True."

"And, um . . . you can call me Violet, if you want."

"Not V?"

"No one calls me V, really. I don't know why I started that."

Milla studies her. Violet fidgets, because it's hard being real instead of fake.

"Violet," Milla says, trying it out. "So cool."

"Why so cool?"

"'Cause 'camilla'—that's my full name—is a flower, too. Did you know that?"

Violet shakes her head.

"It's, like, this tiny white flower that grows by streams." Camilla blushes. She seems, suddenly, to wish she'd kept quiet. "Sometimes they're pink. So, um … yeah."

The corners of Violet's mouth go up, and if Modessa would go ahead and return Tally, then practically the whole world would be made of sunshine.

Well, maybe after the presentations. In the meantime …

Violet smiles at Milla. "So we're both flowers. Awesome."

Twenty-two

Katie-Rose

Katie-Rose is so super-psyched when she gets home Wednesday afternoon. She's buzzing, that's how psyched she is! First, chatting with Milla in the computer lab went awesomely. Awesometatiously awesomely. It was as if the old Milla from Pioneer Camp came back from the dead and took over the body of the Popular Milla from school. It was still Popular Milla's body—authentic Greek *chitōn* paired with glittery, green, completely inauthentic Greek scarf with little pink flowers on the ends—but with the real Milla inside.

And this time, unlike yesterday on the playground, the real Milla didn't stare at her sneakers and say, "Not now." This time, the real Milla smiled.

Sure, the dingleberry comment maybe wasn't Katie-Rose's shining moment. But it wasn't a *disaster*.

Oh, well, dingleberries happen, Katie-Rose thinks, and giggles. That would make a great bumper sticker.

And then . . . *then*! Katie-Rose filmed all of the fifth graders' Greek Week presentations, and she got some fabulous footage, she just knows it. Like with Natalia and the penith? *Oh. My. Gosh.*

Katie-Rose should probably spend some time editing the footage before posting it on BlahBlahSomethingSomething.com, but she's got to prepare for Potato Olympics tomorrow. Greek Week is ker-azy! But fun. Anyway, she can edit it later—maybe add some effects, maybe do certain scenes in old-timey black and white—and then replace the unedited version with the edited version. Or! Ooo, ooo, even better! She can leave the original footage up and title it "Greek Week, Original and Uncut." The edited version can be "Greek Week, the Collector's Edition."

Or maybe the uncut version should be the collector's version? Because don't collectors collect the versions of movies that are rarer and less mainstream? Hmm, and technically, if she uses "Greek Week" in the title, she should incorporate footage from more than just today . . .

So many possibilities, so little time . . . especially with a potato to train. Her mom (*good mommy!*) bought a bag of potatoes at Publix, and Katie-Rose plans to select the biggest, strongest, and most able of the bunch. She will name him Potato von Schnitzel-Fritzle, though he will go by Carl. He will be competing in the luge.

So. Yes. She'll upload what she's got so far, and it'll be . . . a work in progress. Of course she'll insist that Yasaman check it out RIGHT AWAY, because all great filmmakers need feedback in order to perfect their art.

She connects her video camera to her laptop and transfers her raw footage to an iMovie file. Then she logs on to BlahBlahSomethingSomething.com (good golly-wolly, they have *got* to rename the site), and goes to the page called Movie Madness. Katie-Rose came up with that name, and she thinks it's quite fab, thanks very much. There, she clicks on Upload Your Video Now!

A message comes up that makes Katie-Rose laugh out loud.

Yes, you, Katie-Rose! Yasaman has typed. Follow these simple instructions, and in one to ten minutes, your masterpiece will be viewable by the world! Or at least by me . . . assuming I figure out what this wacky "internet" business is all about.

+twists finger in cheek+ "What's the internet, Katie-Rose?" (JK! I'm just teasing you! You know that, right?)

Katie-Rose likes being teased by Yasaman, because Yasaman teases out of love. And Katie-Rose is pretty darn impressed with the ease of Yasaman's setup. She hits Browse to find her footage, and then she clicks Upload. Easy-peasy, simple as pie.

Before jogging downstairs to spend some quality time with Carl, Katie-Rose does one last thing. She sends Yasaman a special "blah-blah" email telling her to go to the Movie Madness page and see what she thinks.

i haven't watched it myself, so you'll be the first to screen it, she types. oh, and i recommend sitting down, cuz it's going to be *epic*.

Twenty-three

Violet's confused, because Modessa never gave Milla Tally the Turtle. She had plenty of opportunities—so why didn't she do it?

And now the school day is over, and everyone has gone home, or to gymnastics or math wizards or whatever. Violet's biting her nails and watching *iCarly*, though she's unable to keep up with the plot. As for Modessa, she's probably at her "Deceit, Guile, and Trickery" class, taught by that Greek chick, Apate.

Ha ha, Violet thinks nervously after coming up with that bit of wit. *Don't be dumb.*

But the question remains: *Why didn't Modessa return Tally?*

Twenty-four

Yasaman

Yasaman sits in front of her computer and sips from a teeny glass of Turkish apple tea, which her mom buys at Akmarket, since it's not sold at Safeway or Publix. She thinks, and not for the first time, that Starbucks should start offering Turkish apple tea, because it is *so good* and not all that different from the Red Passion iced tea they serve. It's just better.

Maybe she'll write a blog post on apple tea after she watches Katie-Rose's video. Katie-Rose's *epic* video, that is. Tee hee. Katie-Rose cracks her up.

Come on, come on, she thinks, watching the spinning

circle that shows the video is loading. It would be cool if she could figure out a way to make that circle less generic and more exciting. Like a hopping frog, maybe? *Hop hop hop* until the video has been streamed and is ready to view?

Ooo, yes, here we go, she thinks, as the static image of Natalia in her Greek horse-riding costume comes to life. Sound blares from the computer, lots of chattering background chaos that sounds exactly like the real, live, chattering background chaos Yasaman hears every day at school. And here it is on her computer!

Yasaman clicks the Full-screen button, and Natalia, gnawing on her lip behind the cage of her enormous headgear, expands until she's practically lifesize. Yasaman jerks back, then remembers *it's just a video* and leans in again.

"The life of a typical tween," Katie-Rose says, her voice overlaying the footage of Natalia typing furiously on her laptop. "A good student—me, for example—would have done her report before the actual moment of the presentations. Alas. I see nothing in this young girl's future save heartbreak and a lifetime dependency on Tums."

Oh, Katie-Rose, Yasaman thinks, giggling. She takes another sip of tea.

"Let's peek in on some others, shall we?" Katie-Rose says, off-screen. The camera pans to Katie-Rose's friend, Max, who is sitting cross-legged and slumpy, his stomach hanging over his dark green shorts. Katie-Rose *tsks*.

"Max has been eating too many cheese puffs," she narrates. "Max is getting a tub. Now, a healthy eater—like *me*, for example . . . well, to be honest, I eat cheese puffs, too."

Yasaman rolls her eyes. Plus, Max is just Max, and he doesn't really have a tub. No more than Yasaman herself does.

". . . fortunate to be blessed with the metabolism of my Chinese forebearers," Katie-Rose is saying as she swings the camera in a wide arc to capture more of what's going on. Yasaman gets a kick out of all the costumes, some awesome and some awful—and . . . oh, look, there's Milla by the water fountain. She's worried about where to sit. That's what her expression says. Her white *chitōn* is super-realistic, though.

The video zooms in on the food table at the far end of

the commons, where there's a tray of baklava—Yasaman never got around to trying any—and a bowl of sliced and sectioned pomegranates. Katie-Rose zooms in tight on one of the pomegranate sections, so that every juice-filled seed stands out in high resolution, like a cluster of deep red jewels.

Nice shot, Yasaman thinks. She's proud of her friend's artistic eye.

Katie-Rose is now speculating about the metabolism of any ancient Greek forebearers she might have had ("... the gyro is a delicacy I certainly enjoy, though not its slimy cousin, the olive ...") but Yasaman is more interested in the slices of life she's treated to as Katie-Rose pulls back from the pomegranate and closes in on Chance, who's actually *dressed* as an olive. *Ha*, Yasaman thinks. How did she miss that during the actual presentations? Preston, who's next to Chance, is poking Chance with a long wooden staff, and Chance doesn't even feel it.

And there's Carmen Glover, who never picks her nose, leaning into her cupped hand and picking away. She withdraws her finger, glances furtively at her classmates, and—

Ew, Yasaman thinks. *Carmen, no.* She makes a note to herself: *Stay away from the area rug with the geometric patterns. Do not ever sit on the area rug with the geometric patterns.*

"Yasaman!" Yasaman's mother calls from the kitchen. "I need your help, *küçüğüm!*" *Küçüğüm* means "my sweet girl," and Yasaman likes being her mother's sweet girl. But right now, she'd rather keep being the fortunate first person to screen Katie-Rose's epic video.

"Just a minute, *Ana!*" she calls.

On the computer screen, something interesting is happening. The shot shows the beat-up sofa where Medusa—*oh, oops*, now Yasaman's doing it herself! *That is so bad*, she tells herself. *Modessa, Modessa, MODESSA.*

The shot is of Modessa dropping down onto her special sofa, since sitting elsewhere would mean sitting *on the floor*, horror of horrors. Quin is with her, of course.

"Observe the cruel Medusa, made of terror," Katie-Rose intones. "To her right, her harpy Quin. I wouldn't get too close, my loyal viewers, for if you do—"

"*Now*, please, Yasaman!" her mother calls. "I want to make *katmer* for your *baba*. I need you to chop the onions!"

Yasaman rises from her desk, keeping her eyes glued on her computer. "Yes, *Ana*! I'm coming, *Ana*!"

Yasaman has missed some of Katie-Rose's commentary, but now Katie-Rose seems to be addressing an actual person rather than her loyal viewers.

"Sure, I can do that," she's saying. "There's a macro setting, see?"

On the screen, the image jumps to a much enlarged shot of Modessa's bottom, and *huh*, there's a hand diving beneath it. It's Modessa's hand, as it turns out, since it's attached to Modessa's arm, which is attached to Modessa's body.

"What about this button?" a male voice says. Yasaman recognizes that voice. It's Mr. Emerson. "What does it do?"

"Oh," Katie-Rose says. "That's how you turn off auto-focus, if for whatever reason you need to take manual control."

From what Yasaman can gather, Katie-Rose was no longer looking at what she was filming. The image of Modessa's bottom jerks, and now it's at a skewed angle. Or maybe Modessa's bottom itself is skewed?

Yep, it sure is. Modessa is for some reason hiking up one bottom cheek, and that hand of hers is fishing around underneath as if something's poking her. Maybe a tack! Or—*ew, yucky!*—maybe one of Carmen Glover's crusty boogers, so dried-up that it's like a hard, spiky sea urchin, hee hee hee.

Oh, this is classic, Yasaman thinks. *Katie-Rose is going to die and go to paradise.*

"Yas-a-*man!*" her mother calls. Her voice is louder than it was. Uh-oh, she's tromping up the stairs. "If I see that you're on the computer . . ."

Ack! Yasaman knows she should turn it off, she needs to turn it off *this second*, but Modessa has found something. She's closing her fingers around it . . . she's pulling it out as her bottom cheek sinks back on the cushion . . .

"*No,*" Yasaman's mother says, reaching past her and snapping off the monitor. She jabs the power button, too, and Yasaman's computer makes a sad *whirrrr* as it shuts down. "No more computer for you, *kiz.*"

"But *Ana*—"

Her mother is firm. "Not for the rest of the night.

Argue, and I will take away tomorrow's privilege as well. Now, come. You have *hamur* to roll out—*and* the onions."

Yasaman casts one last longing look at her computer, whose screen is as blank as an unseeing eye. Then she follows her mother to the kitchen, where the onions await.

THURSDAY, AUGUST 27TH

It's the beginning of the school day, and Camilla can't shake the feeling that V—no, *Violet*—is staring at her. And the reason she can't shake the feeling that Violet's staring at her is because Violet *is* staring at her. *There!* See? Just like the first day of school. Violet was staring *right at her*, and then she jerked her eyes away the second Milla met her gaze.

But why? Weren't they . . . kinda . . . friends now? Yesterday during the Greek presentations, they had so much fun. Milla was expecting Violet to be full of fun again this morning. To tell the truth, she was counting on it. She'd even prepared a "bewitching girdle" remark to toss out oh-so-casually, if the opportunity presented itself.

Stop staring at me like that, Milla mentally tells Violet. *You can talk to me if you want. You can come over and use your silly voice and then grin in that way you have, where all of a sudden your face changes and you look full of mischief. But stop staring at me like something's wrong.*

Milla doesn't like it when things go wrong . . . but the problem is, there are so many things—at school, at home, at Macy's shoe department, even—that *can* go wrong.

Tainted peanut butter. Flying hot tubs. Lost turtles.

She's doing it again, Milla's radar tells her. And sure enough, a peek from beneath a swoop of hair confirms it: Violet's light-brown eyes, almost amber, are locked on hers. They're stunning, Violet's eyes, but right now they make Milla think of aliens. Has an alien possessed Violet, and that's why her stare is so intense?

Being possessed by an alien, that definitely counts as something going wrong. And aliens *could* exist. Milla doesn't doubt it for an instant. The world is rarely as it seems: There could be aliens scuttling like cockroaches underneath anybody's skin, operating that person's body like a robot, and no one would know it except another alien.

Violet is not an alien, she tells herself firmly, and she startles herself by abruptly rising from her desk, striding to Violet, and saying, "What?!"

Violet is startled, too. Her almost-amber eyes widen, and she says, "What do you mean, *what*?"

"Why are you staring at me?" Milla asks.

"I'm staring at you?"

Milla cocks her head. "Do I look weird? Do I . . . have food in my teeth?" She knows she doesn't. She is very thorough about brushing her teeth before school. But what else could it be?

Violet blushes. "Sorry. No. I don't know why I was staring."

"Oh," Milla says. "Well . . . are you mad at me?"

"No! Why would I be?"

"I don't know," Milla says, but she feels better hearing Violet say out loud that she isn't.

"Well, I'm not," Violet says.

"Good."

"Are you . . . mad at *me*?" Violet asks.

Suddenly, this whole exchange strikes Milla as funny. "*No*. Why would I be?"

"Good question," Violet says. She smiles. It's a tentative smile, but a smile nonetheless, and it makes her look so much less like a possible victim of alien possession.

"So . . . um . . . how're things?" Violet asks. She draws her thumb to her mouth and raises her eyebrows, like she truly wants to know.

Milla shrugs. "Good. You?"

"Oh, I'm, uh . . . I'm nothing. I'm great. I was just wondering how *you* are." She sits up straighter, looking more and more like herself with every passing second. "Any exciting new developments in your life?"

At the front of the room, Mr. Emerson has begun his let's-get-started routine, which involves sitting on the front edge of his desk and clearing his throat.

"Does having a pet potato count?" Milla says.

Violet grins. It's the quick-flashing mischievous grin, and it makes Milla happy. "Hmm. Does it do any tricks?"

"Take your seats, please," Mr. Emerson says. "Max, you've sharpened enough pencils."

"But—" Max says.

"Sit down. You, too, Milla."

Milla says bye to Violet by making a goofy expression, then glances over at Max, who's having a struggle abandoning the pencil sharpener. Milla knows from Pioneer Camp that Max is Katie-Rose's neighbor, and that they're friends. Also, based on Katie-Rose's anecdotes, she knows he's a nice guy. A little . . . odd, but nice.

"*Max*," Mr. Emerson warns.

Max looks pained. He's got a whole handful of pencils, and less than half of them have sharp tips. One of the unsharpened ones is worse than simply unsharpened. It's broken off at the top with no lead showing at all, and Milla knows how disconcerting that is.

He holds it up so that Mr. Emerson can see, and says, beseechingly, "Can I just . . . ?"

Mr. Emerson regards Max as if he is a trial. Milla knows he doesn't mean it, though. "All right, Max. Sharpen it and *sit down*."

As Milla slides into her seat, she ducks her head to hide her smile. She (secretly, privately, *totally* confidentially) thinks Max is kinda cute.

Twenty-six

Katie-Rose

"When I call your name, you may get your potato and come to the front of the class," Ms. Perez says to her class. Katie-Rose thinks she looks really cute today. She's wearing a funky turquoise dress with diagonal ruffles along the bottom, and since it's a dress and not pants, no meanies could trash-talk about her . . . *undergarments* . . . even if they wanted to.

Ms. Perez scans the room. "Who would like to go first?"

Katie-Rose's hand shoots up. In an extremely bizarre twist, Modessa's does, too. Katie-Rose doesn't get it. Why does Modessa want to go first? Modessa never wants to go first. Modessa never wants to go, period.

"Modessa," Ms. Perez says, surprised. "Terrific."

Modessa rises from her desk and saunters to the back of the room, where each fifth grader has a hook for jackets and a cubby for backpacks, messenger bags, and random other stuff. The cubbies are organized alphabetically, so Katie-Rose's cubby is in between Yasaman's (yay!) and Modessa's (un-yay).

It takes Modessa *a long time* to get out her potato. Katie-Rose shares a look with Yasaman. She even has time to whisper, "Hey, did you like my video?"

Yasaman nods. "I didn't get to watch it all, but what I saw, yeah. It's awesome."

"Modessa?" Ms. Perez prompts.

Katie-Rose cranes her neck over her shoulder. Why is Modessa standing so near Katie-Rose's cubby? *Step away,* Katie-Rose says in her head. She doesn't want Medusa germs jumping onto her stuff.

"Ready," Modessa says, pivoting on her heel and giving Ms. Perez a smile. Ms. Perez, who doesn't know Modessa made fun of her underwear, smiles back.

Potato in hand, Modessa goes to the front of the room. "This is Tate-Tate," she announces. Tate-Tate has blue magic marker eyes and inch-long black eyelashes. Her lips—it's clearly a girl—are pursed and pink. "Tate-Tate is going to compete in ladies gymnastics."

Modessa nods at Tate-Tate. "Okay, Tate-Tate, let's do it."

She throws Tate-Tate into the air. Tate-Tate goes up, up, up . . . and then down, down, down.

Splat.

The class laughs. Modessa is pleased in her cooler-than-thou way.

"I never said she was any good," she says.

"I'd like to see you put a tad more effort into it next time, Modessa," Ms. Perez says dryly. "Clean up your mess and return to your seat."

See? Katie-Rose tells Ms. Perez mentally. *Told you she was a bad egg.*

"Who's next?" Ms. Perez says, scanning the room.

Katie-Rose's arm zings back into the air. Her fingers stretch yogalike to the ceiling, as do her eyebrows.

"Katie-Rose," Ms. Perez says.

Katie-Rose hops up and goes to her cubby. Modessa's

back there, too, dumping Tate-Tate's remains into the trash can. *Poor Tate-Tate,* Katie-Rose thinks. *She didn't deserve to get Modessa as a trainer.*

Katie-Rose wiggles her backpack out of the cubby, unzips the main portion, and pulls out Potato von Schnitzel-Fritzle (who goes by Carl).

She makes sure Carl's little knitted hat (made from a sock) is in place, then grabs his sled (an old toy truck borrowed from Max) and several rubber bands to get him strapped up.

"Oh my *God,*" Modessa says, hovering behind her.

Katie-Rose rolls her eyes. *Yes, I put effort into my presentation. Yes, I enjoy school. So?*

Except, the next thing she knows, Modessa is shoving her aside—*what the . . . ?*—and snatching her backpack.

"Hey!" Katie-Rose exclaims.

Modessa marches to Ms. Perez's desk, holding Katie-Rose's backpack by the top loop like it's a dead rat. She thunks it on Ms. Perez's desk.

"Look inside," Modessa commands. "Just *look.*"

Katie-Rose is baffled. Yasaman glances at her, her expression a question. Katie-Rose lifts her shoulders.

At the front of the room, Ms. Perez frowns and pulls open the front of Katie-Rose's backpack. She peers inside.

What did I do? Katie-Rose wonders. *Did I forget to turn something in? Am I not allowed to have gel pens?*

Ms. Perez lifts her head and looks at Katie-Rose, who gets a bad feeling in her stomach.

"Katie-Rose?" she says in a tone no teacher has ever used with her.

"Y-yes?" Katie-Rose says.

Modessa takes over, thrusting her hand into Katie-Rose's backpack and pulling out a red-and-orange bobble-head turtle. She holds it up for everyone to see.

"Katie-Rose stole Camilla's turtle!" she accuses. Katie-Rose's arms go slack, and she drops Carl and all his equipment. *"Katie-Rose is a thief!"*

Twenty-seven

Camilla

Milla can't stop crying. It's afternoon break, and she and Modessa are off by themselves, and she can't. Stop. Crying.

"I just . . ." Milla breaks off. *Ack*, it's like she's some baby who can't control her own emotions.

She squeezes her fingers tight around Tally the Turtle. *Tally is safe. Tally is back. Tally is solid and real and here in her hand.* That's what she needs to remember.

Still . . .

"I don't understand *why*," she says, finally getting the sentence out with only a little wobbling.

"No one does, sweetie," Modessa says. The two of them are hiding inside a pink-and-white plastic playhouse, which is against the rules since older kids aren't supposed to be in the preschool area. But the preschoolers are taking their naps, and the pink-and-white playhouse is the safest place Milla can think of.

Its refrigerator is stocked with plastic hamburgers and pickles and hot dogs that come out of their buns. There's no running water, but there's a sink. There are chunky blue shutters on the windows, and Milla remembers being a preschooler and pushing the shutters open so that the playhouse could serve as a snack shack. Kids would place their orders from outside the window, and Milla would put a cookie or whatever on the thick windowsill and say, "Here you go, ma'am. Would you like some lemonade to go with it?"

The lemonade was sand scooped into a cup.

"Obviously, she's obsessed with you," Modessa says.

"Huh?" Milla says. She kinda went into her own world there for a sec.

"Katie-*Rose*," Modessa says, giving Milla a strange look. She stretches her legs out so that they're flush with

Milla's. Their feet nearly reach the opposite wall of the playhouse.

"But what I don't get," Modessa goes on, "is why she thought stealing your turtle would bring you two closer."

Milla doesn't respond. When Modessa first returned Tally, Tally was cold. Milla sandwiched her in her palms while Modessa relayed the whole sordid Potato Olympics story, and by the time Modessa was done, Tally was warm again and felt almost alive.

"Katie-Rose has never stolen anything before," Milla says.

"That you know of," Modessa points out.

"Maybe she just *found* her," Milla says. "Maybe she found her and was going to give her back to me, but just hadn't gotten a chance yet."

"Hmm," Modessa says. She drums her fingers on the playhouse's pretend-wood floor, which, like the walls, is made of white plastic and doesn't look like wood at all. "Well, did you see her today? Before Potato Olympics?"

Milla's face falls. "In the hall as I was going to class, yeah. And . . ."

"And what?"

"And she smiled and said 'hi.'" She looks at Modessa imploringly. "Why would she be all nice like that if the whole time she had Tally?"

Modessa opens her mouth, then shuts it and shakes her head. Whatever mean thing she was going to say, she's bitten it back, and Milla is grateful.

"Listen," Modessa says. "The thing is . . ."

Or maybe she's going to say it now, Milla thinks.

"What?" she says.

Modessa tilts her foot so that her black sandal touches Milla's white sneaker. "Katie-Rose, she's always been . . . well . . . a foster friend anyway, right?"

Milla's face heats up. Modessa made that term up last year to describe girls who hung around and hung around because they didn't have friends of their own. Girls you were nice to—girls *Milla* was nice to—but who just didn't belong.

Katie-Rose was more than a foster friend at Pioneer Camp, Milla thinks. *More than a foster friend in the computer lab yesterday.*

"I wonder if she just wanted a part of you," Modessa

says. She watches Milla carefully. "Because she wanted to be your friend so bad? And you . . . well, *you* know. It's not like you opened up the welcome wagon for her."

Milla's tears start up again.

"I'm not saying it's your fault. I'm totally not saying that," Modessa says.

"You didn't *want* me to be nice to her!" Milla says.

"I didn't want her to be a Panda," Modessa corrects.

But isn't that the same thing? Milla wonders. *Can you be nice to someone and still have a not-so-secret secret club that you don't let them into?*

Tears roll down Milla's cheeks, and she is tangled and confused and lonely and *bad*.

Modessa hugs her, which means a lot, because Modessa as a rule doesn't go for touching. "Milla . . . do you want me to get Katie-Rose back for you?"

Get Katie-Rose back? Milla thinks foggily. Her brain plays with the words, because they mean such different things depending on how you interpret them.

Get her back: make her pay.

Get her back: find her and return her.

But Milla knows which meaning Modessa has in mind. She sniffles and says, "No. I mean, *thanks* . . . but no."

Modessa awkwardly pats Milla's shoulder, while Milla holds Tally tight.

Twenty-eight

Yasaman

As soon as she gets home, Yasaman marches straight to her computer.

No, that's not true. As soon as Yasaman gets home

- and takes off her *hijab*
- and fixes Nigar a snack
- and unloads the dishwasher for her mom
- and cleans out Blackberry's litter box
- and starts a fresh load of laundry
- and serves her mother a small cup of strong Turkish coffee while her mother sinks onto the sofa and allows herself a small break for her soap opera . . .

After doing all that, *then* Yasaman marches straight to her computer.

"Thank you, Yasaman," her mother calls as Yasaman heads upstairs. "You are my *melek*."

"You're welcome," Yasaman calls back.

In her bedroom, Yasaman powers up her computer. She logs on to BlahBlahSomethingSomething.com and opens her journal. Post an Entry? is one of the options. All riled up inside, she clicks *Yes*.

I don't like mean people, she types. Mean people should go away and never come back. Mean people should remember that there are BIG HORRIBLE THINGS IN THE WORLD ALREADY, like starvation and lost pets and captured soldiers being tortured. They should remember that and not make the world WORSE.

Yasaman pauses, paralyzed by the awareness of how much she's saying from her heart. It can be dangerous, speaking from your heart.

But it can be even more dangerous to turn away from your heart, she reminds herself. Anyway, she'll set this journal entry to "private," meaning that she'll be the only one able to see it.

Modessa did something bad. She made everyone think Katie-Rose stole Tally the Turtle, but I *know* Katie-Rose didn't.

Yasaman remembers Milla's tear-swollen face at pickup, how she wouldn't make eye contact with anyone. She remembers how scared Katie-Rose looked as she said, "Camilla, *no*, you've got to believe me!"

And then Modessa appeared by Milla's side, and Quin was right behind her, and they squeezed Katie-Rose out without touching her or talking to her and acknowledging her existence.

Yasaman repositions her hands over the keyboard.

I know Modessa had something to do with it, because I heard her and that new girl talking in the bathroom. They were talking about Milla and Katie-Rose. *And* Tally the Turtle.

Did Modessa plant the turtle in Katie-Rose's backpack to frame her?

Or, wait. Did the new girl do it?!!!

Maybe . . . but only if Modessa told her to, Yasaman suspects. She flashes back to what she overheard in the bathroom:

"*What worries me is that she's just not making good decisions,*" Modessa said to V. The "she" they were discussing was Milla. "*I mean, she was talking to* Katie-Rose. *She was* laughing *with Katie-Rose! The very day after Katie-Rose called me . . . what she called me!*"

Yasaman understands why Modessa got mad when Katie-Rose called her "Medusa," and the possibility of Modessa trying to get revenge doesn't surprise her. She expected it, to tell the truth. But was Modessa so heartless that she'd blame a *robbery* on her? Was V so heartless that she'd go along with it—*if* she had anything to do with it?

To Yasaman, all interpretations seem ridiculous. Ridiculous and even . . . *pathetic*, so maybe she has it all wrong. Especially since by blaming Katie-Rose for stealing Tally the Turtle, Modessa wasn't just hurting Katie-Rose. She was hurting Milla, too. *Definitely* hurting Milla.

Yasaman takes a breath.

Everything Allah created is good, she types. The bad in the world comes from the bad that's inside humans. From *Shaitan*, the devil.

Yasaman's fingers hover over the keyboard, because there's more she wants to say. Then she sticks them under her thighs, because saying it—typing it—would make it more real than if she just . . . doesn't.

There's a knock on Yasaman's door. It's a politeness knock, since closed doors aren't allowed in Yasaman's house.

"Yasaman?" her little sister says.

Yasaman clicks Save as Private, puts the computer to sleep so that nothing's visible on the screen, and swivels in her desk chair.

"Hey, Nigar," she says. She forces a smile. "Come on in."

Nigar does. She's so adorable, her almost-four-year-old sister who's a "big girl now" because she goes to preschool. Her hair is in glossy pigtails tied with pink bows, because Nigar loves bows. Just last night Nigar proudly told Yasaman and her parents that she is known in her preschool class as "the girl who always wears bows."

"It's my trademark," Nigar said, and their dad laughed. Nigar has beautiful hair, so why not wear bows? She's not old enough to don a *hijab*.

"Will you play with me?" Nigar asks Yasaman now. Nigar's voice is sad, which sends warning bells dinging and blaring in Yasaman's head. Nigar is made of sunshine. She's hardly ever sad.

"What's wrong?" Yasaman asks. She pulls Nigar onto her lap. Such a sweet, warm, cinnamon-smelling girl, her sister. "Did something happen at school?"

"I don't like Rivendell," Nigar says.

"Yes you do. You love Rivendell."

Nigar wiggles to get better access to Yasaman's hair, which she finger-combs. Nigar loves playing with Yasaman's hair. Yasaman loves it, too. It makes her feel like a chimp having the nits picked out of her fur . . . but in a good way.

"Nigar?" Yasaman says, regarding her sister from behind the locks of hair Nigar has pulled in front of Yasaman's face.

Nigar strokes and separates. Her expression is forlorn. But she doesn't respond, and Yasaman doesn't push it. Nigar will speak when she's ready.

Twenty-nine

Violet

iolet gets the big pair of scissors from the kitchen. Her mother used to use them when she cooked, which Violet thought was funny. She'd laugh as her mom snipped florets off a head of broccoli, and her mom would laugh, too. "What?" she'd say. "It's easier than using a knife."

But Violet isn't borrowing (stealing?) the kitchen shears to make a side of steamed broccoli. Anyway, is it "stealing" to take the shears from the kitchen? No. Is it "stealing" to spot a toy turtle in the school hallway, pick it up, and then—eventually—put it back down beneath a sofa cushion?

Violet hates Modessa for accusing Katie-Rose of being a thief. *Hates* her. She hates herself, too, for the role she played in letting it happen. *If I had just given Tally back to Milla on Monday...*

Someone, probably Quin, made a sign today and taped it to Katie-Rose's locker: IN THE OLDEN DAYS, THIEVES HAD THEIR HANDS CUT OFF, it said.

Violet checked to make sure no one was watching, then ripped it off and threw it away.

Now, Violet takes the scissors upstairs to her bedroom. She stands with them in front of her mirror. Why? Because, as a person, Violet sucks. She could have kept all this from happening, but she didn't... and if she's that ugly on the inside, she might as well be ugly on the outside.

(stop it. you're acting crazy.)

And that's a surprise?! Craziness runs in your blood, stupid.

Her mom went crazy, kinda, and now she lives in a nice little ward with nice little locks on the nice little doors. If she earns enough points, she's allowed out on the nice little lawn to play croquet. If she earns even more points, Violet might get to play croquet with her one day. *Happy happy joy joy.*

(miss you so much, Mom. miss you so—)

Violet slaps her own face. She slaps it *hard*. She grabs a chunk of her hair, lifts the scissors, and opens the blades. *Hungry, hungry hippos*, she thinks absurdly.

"Violet?" she hears. Her dad's home from work.

Do it, she tells herself. Her heart pounds. There are fast breaths in her chest.

"I brought us a home-cooked meal," her dad says. His feet thump the stairs. "Well, close to home-cooked. I found a place called the Supper Fork. Every day, they whip up something fresh."

Do it. Chop off your hair, ugly girl.

(no)

"Does lasagna sound good?" her dad asks. He's at the top of the stairs. He's almost to the bathroom. "I also got garlic bread and a side of broccoli."

LIKE BROCCOLI, SEE? DO IT.

(no! stop yelling at me!)

Her dad raps on her door. "Vi?"

She puts down the scissors and whips around, just as her dad sticks his head in the room.

"I got chocolate lava cake, too," he says. He grins, strides across the room, and gives Violet a hug. "How does *that* sound?"

Violet breathes in the pine tree smell of his after-shave. She squeezes him tight, tight, tight.

Her dad chuckles. "Wow, you must really be sick of burgers."

"I am," she says. It comes out a little hiccupy, and her dad pulls her closer.

"Aw, Violet," he says, all laughter gone. He sways with her in his arms. It's like being rocked. After a minute, he steps back, takes her chin, and tilts her head.

"I'm so glad you're my girl," he says, and Violet can see it in his eyes, can see his crazy-fierce love for her that will never, ever go away.

Violet tears up. *This* is what she needed, she realizes: not to wallow in self-hatred, but to remember that she's lovable. And if she's lovable, that means there's beauty in her somewhere, even if it's been sort of . . . shriveled up lately.

Beauty is as beauty does, however. That was something her mom liked to say.

Violet presses back into her dad's chest. As he wraps his arms around her, she makes herself a promise: *Tomorrow at school, I'll find a way to make things right.*

Thirty

Katie-Rose

*P*lease be online, Katie-Rose prays as she clicks
the Refresh button for the gazillionth time. *Please
please please*. Yasaman hasn't been online for the last
hour, and if Yasaman's giving her the silent treatment,
too, then Katie-Rose will die.

A spinning circle appears on the BlahBlahSome-
thingSomething.com homepage to let Katie-Rose know
that, yes, the page is being refreshed. When the spinning
circle disappears, the homepage is exactly the same. There
is no cheerful message reading, "Yasaman is online!"

"*Ag*," Katie-Rose's babysitter says. Her name is Chrissy,

and she goes to high school with Yasaman's cousin, Hulya. She's giving herself a manicure while watching a rerun of *Ugly Betty* on her own laptop. "Boo. *Bad!*"

Dully, Katie-Rose looks over at her. "What's wrong?" she says.

Chrissy makes a face and holds up her hand, nails toward Katie-Rose. Four of the five look pretty, but Chrissy's thumb is smeared with orange.

"I suck at self-manicures," Chrissy says. "Come help me."

"Well . . . I'm kinda not—"

Chrissy groans. Chrissy is *very* dramatic. Chrissy also comes up with the nuttiest, most wonderful ideas ever, like sumo wrestling with pillows tied to their bellies. The two of them did that once, and it was a blast, although Katie-Rose has a hard time recalling that emotion now.

"I look like a smushed, pulpy, disgusting pumpkin," Chrissy complains. "My *thumb* looks like a smushed, pulpy, disgusting pumpkin. *Please* come help me, Katie-Rose."

Katie-Rose sighs. She's not in the mood for manicures, but it's not as if she's in the mood for anything else, either. *Maybe if I go away for a few minutes, Yasaman'll*

get online, she thinks. She slides off her computer chair and joins Chrissy on the floor.

"Thank you, dahlink," Chrissy says in a fancy-lady voice. She pushes over her manicure kit. "You have *no* idea."

First, Katie-Rose takes off Chrissy's gloppy polish. It's so vivid that it takes multiple wipes to remove it all.

"Hey, um, Chrissy?"

"Yeah?"

"Have you ever . . . did you ever . . ."

"Spit it out, small fry," Chrissy says, then grins because it's a funny term, *small fry*. Katie-Rose gives a flat smile in return. Chrissy is one grade above her oldest brother, Charlie, but unlike Charlie, Chrissy never treats Katie-Rose like a baby.

Right now, Charlie and Sam are at karate and Katie-Rose's parents are at a charity benefit. That's why Chrissy is here. Katie-Rose could, technically, babysit herself, but Katie-Rose thinks that's too freaky, the idea of being alone in their big, huge house.

"Have you ever had . . . friend problems?" Katie-Rose says. She immediately busies herself with the bottle of Tangerine Dream nail polish, because *der*. Of course

Chrissy has never had friend problems. Chrissy is bubbly and blonde and über-confident—who wouldn't want to be friends with her?

"Are you kidding?" Chrissy says. "All the time."

Katie-Rose lifts her head. "Really?"

"Oh my God. You don't even want to know." She tilts her head. "Like, Francesca? Who's friends with me and Chelsea, but doesn't get along with Hulya? Just today Francesca told Chelsea that Hulya's after this guy, Jellico, which she totally isn't, unless it *happens* to turn out that Jellico likes her already. I'm trying to find out for her. But Chelsea isn't dating Jellico! She just has a crush on him. Is it illegal for Hulya to like him, too?"

"Um . . ."

"Francesca was being totally backstabby to bring it up. Now, if Hulya and Jellico start going *out* . . ." Chrissy lets her sentence trail off meaningfully. "You see what I'm saying?"

Um, no, Katie-Rose doesn't. Still, it helps to know that other people have problems.

Has anyone ever accused you of being a thief? she wants to ask. But she would never.

"So what do you do?" she asks instead. "To fix things?"

Chrissy lets out a *pffffff*. "Yeah, right. *Ha*. Fix things—I wish."

There's a pause, and Katie-Rose figures that's it. There's no more to her answer. They'll just watch *Ugly Betty* together . . . and she guesses that's not so bad.

But as she carefully applies polish to Chrissy's thumbnail, Chrissy starts up again.

"You know what's hard?" she says.

"What?"

"My *sister*."

"You have a sister?" Katie-Rose says. "I didn't know that."

"Yeah, Angela. She's a freshman at the University of Georgia. She's never here, that's why you've never met her."

Katie-Rose detects pride in Chrissy's tone, but also something else. She finishes the first coat and blows on Chrissy's thumb, watching Chrissy's face.

"She's perfect, is all," Chrissy says. "I mean, not exactly as a *person*—"

"Why is she not perfect as a person?" Katie-Rose asks. This is getting slightly fascinating enough to temporarily distract Katie-Rose from her own hornets' nest of problems.

Chrissy rolls her eyes, as if there are so many reasons her sis isn't perfect. "She's ditzy. She's a spaz. She let a guy give her a Jeep once, when she didn't even *like* him—and then she gave it back! Can you believe it?"

"A *Jeep*?"

"Oh, and there was this whole thing with chickens, and this stuffed animal named Boo Boo Bear, and then there was my aunt who got into this *pole-dancing* ring ..." Chrissy raises her eyebrows. "That's who Angela lives with in Atlanta, our aunt Sadie. Only Angela's not there so much now that she's in college. *You* know."

Again, Katie-Rose actually doesn't. Her head is spinning. Chickens? Boo Boo Bear? *Pole dancing?*

"It's a long story," Chrissy says. "But the point is, Angela may be a total ditz—even though I love her! *Totally* love her. But the one thing she's *never* had to deal with is friend problems. And you want to know why?"

Chrissy looks at Katie-Rose, waiting. Katie-Rose waits, too, anxious about what she's going to hear.

"Because Angela's friends are *rock solid*."

"Oh."

"Yyyyep."

Chrissy wiggles her fingers to remind Katie-Rose that it's time for the second coat. As Katie-Rose paints, Chrissy tells her all about Angela and her two best buds, Zoe and Maddie. The way Chrissy makes it sound, Angela, Zoe, and Maddie are really cool, really tight, and never ever *ever* let anything come between them, even though they're living apart from each other for the first time in their lives, since they all go to different colleges.

"But if they're all at different colleges, how do they . . . stay tight?" Katie-Rose asks. She feels silly using that term, but grown-up, too.

Chrissy shrugs. "The internet."

Katie-Rose startles. The internet! Yasaman! She applies one last stroke of polish to Chrissy's nail, then recaps the bottle and jumps to her feet. "There you go. Gotta get back to work now."

"Uh, okay," Chrissy says. "Thanks. But do you see what I mean about how it's a drag to have friend problems when my sister never does?"

"Uh-huh!" Katie-Rose calls out. She drops into her

computer chair, checks herself from rolling backward, and clicks the Refresh button. She squeezes shut her eyes for three seconds. Then she squinch-opens her right eye. Blurry. She squinch-opens her left—still blurry—then gives in and opens both eyes wide.

Yasaman is online! announces the alert at the top of the page.

Relief courses through her. She types like a maniac.

Chat with Yasaman	
The*rose*knows:	yasaman, u there?
Yasaman:	katie-rose! omigosh, i'm so glad to hear from u!
The*rose*knows:	u r? why? cuz i'm a pariah, u know. i tried to talk to milla at pickup and she refused to look me in the eye.
The*rose*knows:	**she wouldn't even _look_ at me!**
The*rose*knows:	but yasaman!!!!! **i did not steal tally the turtle!!!!**
Yasaman:	i know
The*rose*knows:	i realize that there r facts supposedly pointing against me. i realize tally was in

	my backpack. **but i swear on all that is holy that i didn't put her there!**
Yasaman:	c above. i know u didn't
The*rose*knows:	wait. u believe me?!
Yasaman:	of course i do
Yasaman:	AND i know who really did it . . . or at least, i think i do. it was modessa
The*rose*knows:	modessa? oh. my. **GOD**
The*rose*knows:	u think she planted tally in my bag? but how?
Yasaman:	well, it's really just a big hunch, based on a lot of stuff. but was there any time today when she could have been near yr backpack, w/o u knowing?
The*rose*knows:	no
The*rose*knows:	**or wait just a minute . . .** yes! there *was* a time, cuz when we were doing our potato olympics, and i went to get potato von schnitzel-fritzle out of my backpack—
Yasaman:	WHO?
The*rose*knows:	potato von schnitzel-fritzle, but u can call him carl. not important

The*rose*knows: but that's when modessa cld have done it!
it makes total sense!!!!!

The*rose*knows: only . . .

Yasaman: only what?

The*rose*knows: how wld modessa have gotten tally in the
first place?

Yasaman: well . . . i think the new girl might have
something to do with it

The*rose*knows: v? the girl who was rude and obnoxious
about ms. perez's underwear?

Yasaman: yeah. sad huh?

Yasaman: but there's even *more* sadness, actually,
only it doesn't have to do with modessa or v.

The*rose*knows: who does it have to do with?

Yasaman: +sighs+ r u sure u wanna go there?

The*rose*knows: um . . . i think so. is everything all right?

Yasaman: not exactly. not for my little sister

The*rose*knows: i know who yr little sis is, i think. always
wears a bow?

Yasaman: yeah, that's nigar

The*rose*knows: nigar?

Yasaman: that's her name. i know what ur thinking,

but it's pronounced nee-GAHR, not . . . the other way. altho ppl always get it wrong, and today 2 boys jumped on her during recess and pounded her spine with their elbows. they kept yelling, "die, nigar, die!"

The*rose*knows: that's terrible! just cuz of her name?

Yasaman: who knows? maybe because of her name, maybe because she looks different?

The*rose*knows: they told her to **die**??? what meanie-butts!

Yasaman: i know. she's 4, katie-rose

Yasaman: i just . . . i feel like a huge pillow of sadness is smushing down and smothering me. i told my parents, and they called nigar's teacher. but nigar's teacher said the boys were just playing a game.

The*rose*knows: yeah, right. doesn't sound like a game to me

Yasaman: well, first the teacher said it was just a game, and then she said fine, she would call the boys' parents and suggest that the boys apologize. only she called my father back later and said both boys refused to say sorry, and that their parents didn't know how to make them.

The*rose*knows: what???

Yasaman: and nigar's just the sweetest little kid, and she LOVED school (at least the first three days of it), and now she's scared to go back.

The*rose*knows: my mom would take away every single privilege i had if i refused to do something she told me to do.

Yasaman: i know. mine 2

The*rose*knows: and that teacher! it makes me so mad that she'd just be like, "oh, kids and their games." !!!!!!

Yasaman: it makes me mad, 2. if only i had PROOF that it wasn't a game, u know? proof that those boys r just bullies.

The*rose*knows: while ur at it, cld u get proof of modessa being a bully 2? like, cold hard proof that no one cld dispute? i know, maybe some glossy 8x10s that show her planting tally in my backpack. happen to have anything like that?

Yasaman: i wish. but . . .

Yasaman: omg. actually . . .

The*rose*knows: what? ur thinking something—tell me!

Yasaman: i'm not thinking anything FOR SURE. i'm just
                thinking about a *maybe*

Yasaman: have u gotten a chance to look over your
                footage from our greek week presentations?

The*rose*knows: um, no. i've been too busy wallowing in
                misery. why?

Yasaman: cuz there's something weird on it. a part
                with modessa—she's sitting on the sofa with
                quin, and i think she found something in the
                cracks between the cushions—

The*rose*knows: OMG, WAS IT TALLY?!!!!

Yasaman: i don't know! it cld have been nothing, but
                i don't know, cuz i had to go help my mom
                with dinner.

The*rose*knows: i'll go look at it right now. i'll get my
                babysitter to help me analyze it, cuz
                chrissy's good with girl drama, she's
                always mixed up in so much of it
                herself.

Yasaman: chrissy who goes to school with my cousin? hulya?

The*rose*knows: yup. chrissy was telling me about hulya just, like, 10 minutes ago, that she's boy-crazy and likes a guy named Jellico.

Yasaman: ha. hulya says it's *chrissy* who's boy crazy and has a crush on jellico.

The*rose*knows: well, maybe they both do.

Yasaman: go look at yr camera footage, k? i'll try to, too. call me IMMEDIATELY if u find anything.

The*rose*knows: what do u mean, u'll "try" to? it's posted right there on yr site, dummy.

Yasaman: yeah, but i'm only allowed half an hour of computer time a day. but promise u'll call, cuz I have a gut feeling about this.

Yasaman: i also have a gut feeling about something else. wanna know?

The*rose*knows: is it good?

Yasaman: VERY good. my gut feeling is that it's time for the good ppl to win for once

The*rose*knows: ahhhhhh. i *like* the way u think.

Yasaman: first c if u have any evidence. then call me!!!!

FRIDAY, AUGUST 28

Thirty-one

Camilla

Why would someone who likes you want to hurt you? That's what Milla wonders as her mom pulls into Rivendell's parking lot on Friday morning. Today Mom Joyce is dropping Milla off, and usually Milla would be thrilled, since Mom Joyce drives a black BMW convertible. Riding in it makes Milla feel like a movie star.

But today, instead of imagining she's Disney's next It Girl, Milla is imagining nothing. Or, no, that's not true. She's imagining things like *nothingness* and *no friends* and *ominous black rain clouds*.

The *no friends* worry is silly—wasn't Modessa so

super-nice to her yesterday when she was all wrecked about Katie-Rose? And even Katie-Rose *wants* to be friends, Milla suspects. Katie-Rose called Milla three times last night, but Milla shook her head each time when Mom Abigail held out the phone.

"Do you want to talk about it?" Mom Abigail said after telling Katie-Rose again that Milla was swamped with homework and suggesting—kindly, but firmly—that she wait and see Milla at school tomorrow.

"No," Milla said.

"Well, she made it seem urgent, whatever it is," Mom Abigail said. She regarded Milla with an expression Milla was familiar with: concerned, but at the same time thinking, *Oh, it's just a kid problem. How urgent can it be?* "She said to log on to some sort of website, that there's something you need to see?"

But Milla didn't, even though she could guess what site Katie-Rose was talking about. She didn't want to deal with it.

Nothing matters, she tells herself now. Sometimes Milla pretends life is just a made-up story, or a dream, and she's merely floating through as an observer. But the fat drop of rain that splats the windshield *is* real, and so is the next one, which lands on Milla's bare arm. Milla sighs, because it's hard to pretend everything's an illusion when the illusion is slopping down and getting you wet.

"Aw, man!" Mom Joyce says good-naturedly. She pulls out of the drop-off line and parks in one of the faculty spaces. "Help me put the top up, will you, babe?"

Getting caught in rainstorms and having to put the top up are two of the many reasons Mom Abigail teases Mom Joyce about owning a convertible. Mom Joyce counters that Mom Abigail is a soccer mom in her bright red minivan, which isn't true, because Milla doesn't play soccer. She takes dance.

But Mom Abigail says *pfff* to Mom Joyce's soccer mom comments, reminding Mom Joyce that a minivan is exactly what she needs for her catering business. "Anyway, I love my bright red minvan," Mom Abigail says breezily. "It reminds me of cherries."

Her moms are so different—and yet they fit together perfectly.

Just like people can be different and still be friends, Milla thinks. *They can be different and still . . . click.*

She closes her eyes and shakes her head. *Of course people can be different and like each other. Duh.*

Why is her brain being so weird?

Why does she click with the girl who stole her turtle, and not click—not really, not in the crazy-snort-giggling way—with Medusa? *Ag. Modessa!!!*

"Mill?" Mom Joyce says. "Rain. Sky." She points at the darkening clouds. "Top up *now*."

"Oh," Milla says. "Right!" She scurries out of the car and helps her mom heave the heavy fabric top into place. It's an old Beemer—a classic, her mom would say— which means Milla and Mom Joyce have to snap snaps and clasp clasps and all sorts of car-ish stuff.

"Thanks, babe," Mom Joyce says. She climbs back in the car. "Kiss?"

Milla kisses her mom's cheek. As she's leaning over, she spots her green sparkly scarf on the passenger seat. It must have fallen off during the ride.

Her mom catches on. She swoops up Milla's scarf and hands it to her.

"Here you go, sweetie," Mom Joyce says. "Today's your ice cream social, right? Hope it doesn't get rained out!" She shifts her Beemer into gear and pulls out of the parking lot.

Milla rubs her thumb over the silky strands of her scarf. It makes her feel melancholy, so instead of looping it around her neck, she swings her backpack off her shoulder, awkwardly unzips the top, and pushes her scarf inside.

It's a good thing, too, because just as she gets her backpack closed, the skies open up. That happens in California sometimes. No rain, no rain, no rain . . . and then *boom*. Milla is soaked before she can even think to make a mad dash for the building. Then, when she manages to get her feet moving, she's nearly hit by a mini-van pulling out of the drop-off lane.

"Oh, hon, I'm so sorry!" the mom in the driver's seat says, rolling her window down an inch. "You've got to watch where you're going!"

"Yes, ma'am," Milla says.

The woman speeds off, and the tires spray muddy water all over Milla.

Milla cries.

Everyone else is in a car, or in the building, and they're

dry and warm and don't have mud on them. Milla *could* get in out of the rain—it's not as if her legs have lost the ability to move—but she's crying, and the rain is plastering her hair all messy over her face, and she's muddy and ugly. *Muggly.* And even though sometimes Milla's fairly good at the whole being-a-functioning-human-being thing ... well, sometimes she's really not.

"Did you know that you get more wet if you run through the rain than if you walk?" somebody says.

Milla's head swivels. It's Max, who likes to sharpen pencils.

"Huh?" Milla says.

"I learned it on *MythBusters*," Max explains. He starts toward the building, and after a moment's pause, Milla falls in with him. She feels like she's not in her own body.

Max continues his monologue. "They kept all factors equal. They used a football stadium, and rigged up overhead sprinklers, and then they did different trials to see who got the wettest."

Milla is focusing more on Max's footsteps than his words, but his words have a nice rhythm. Even if she has no idea what he's talking about.

"They wore special suits made of . . . of . . ." He makes a sound of frustration. "What were they *made* of?"

Max's steady pace has brought them almost to the building's overhang. Other kids are mad-dashing to shelter. There are more car-door-slamming sounds than usual.

"At any rate, the scientists were able to measure the amount of water that got on them," Max says. "That's the point. And when they *ran*, they got wetter, because their bodies came into contact with more raindrops. Does that make sense?"

"But walking is slower."

At last they reach the overhang. "Doesn't matter," Max says. "Less drops hit you overall."

"But . . . people always run to get out of the rain."

"*You* didn't," Max says.

"Well, that's because . . ." Her sentence trickles off. Why didn't she?

She frowns and looks down at herself. She's drenched. She's no doubt tearstained. Her white jeans are splattered with mud, and her white shirt is also splattered with mud. Plus, it's clammy, and it clings see-through thin against her body. With a jolt, she wraps her arms around herself.

"It's like—okay, imagine this," Max says. "You know how when you're going somewhere in a car? And it's raining? But whenever you stop at a stoplight, it seems to rain less?"

What am I going to do? Milla thinks. *How can I go inside with my shirt all see-through?*

"Well, it doesn't rain *less* when you stop," Max goes on. "The amount of rain coming down stays constant. All that matters is how fast or slow you're going as you move through it."

He looks at Milla, and his eyebrows pull together. "Are you okay?"

How do you tell a boy that your shirt is transparent and you can't go inside? Milla wonders. *You can't. There is no way to say those words.*

Tears threaten to overflow.

"You're really wet," Max says. He pauses. "You're way wetter than I am."

"I stood there longer," Milla replies, sniffling. She doesn't want him thinking his running-versus-walking theory is wrong just because she stood stockstill like a dummy.

"Yeah, you were kind of on a time delay, only no one had programmed in a rain sensor."

"Huh?"

"Like with the NXT robot I helped build for our robotics competition. We needed it to roll forward—that was one of the required tasks—but not until a specific amount of time had elapsed. So we programmed in a sound sensor, and when Thomas blew a whistle, the robot rolled forward approximately a foot and a half to knock over—"

Milla has understood none of this. But now, out of the blue, Max's jaw drops open and he's no longer talking, period.

"Max?"

He closes his mouth with a snap. When he opens it to speak, his words tumble out in a rush. "Oh man! I just figured out how to make my domino course work!"

"You use dominoes in robotics?"

He draws his eyebrows together. "No. I do robotics in robotics. I do dominoes at my house, and I've been working on a course that incorporates five hundred dominoes."

"That's ... a lot of dominoes," Milla says.

"I've been seriously questioning it, though," Max continues, "because there's one section I haven't been able to figure out. The dominoes build up too much momentum, that's the problem, and their trajectory becomes unpredictable. But if I could let that one section expend its energy—and program an NXT with a time delay that's triggered by the sound of falling dominoes ..."

He's adorable when he gets excited, Milla thinks. Too bad the world is so sad. She's glad he can be happy, though. Even if such happiness is no longer within her reach.

"Thanks, Milla," Max says. "Thanks a ton. I'd have never figured it out if you weren't so wet."

Milla smiles ruefully. He's adorable, yes. But his social skills could use a little work.

"Hey, I have my robotics shirt in my backpack," he says. "You can wear it if you want."

Max squats, unzips his backpack, and pulls out

a hand-painted blue T-shirt. It's not at all the kind of shirt Milla would make if she had puff paint and fabric markers and a lovely shirt to decorate. Max's shirt has a black rectangle on it with white antennae. There are gray squiggles beneath the rectangle (is the rectangle supposed to be a robot?), and laser beams or something shooting out from its body.

GO MIGHTY TERMITES! the shirt says in messy letters.

Max offers it to Milla, and Milla accepts. She pulls it on over her soaked one.

"It looks nice," Max says, cocking his head.

"Yeah?" Max's robotics shirt is, bar none, the ugliest shirt she's ever seen, yet her heart swells at his compliment. "Thanks," she says, blushing.

Thirty-two

Yasaman

asaman has always been good at eaves-dropping, and she's only getting better. Maybe she'll be a spy when she grows up. Or . . . why wait? Maybe she'll be a spy now, and wear cute plaid uniform skirts and knee-highs like the girls in Yasaman's favorite book series. Those girls aren't much older than Yasaman, and they go to an actual spy school. They know karate and have cool gadgets and swishy, shiny hair.

None of them wears a *hijab*, though. And of course Yasaman's *baba* would never let her wear a plaid uniform skirt.

So, Yasaman will settle for being stealthy-sneakered invisi-girl, *mwahaha*. There are perks to being the quiet Muslim girl no one sees—well, except when she trips, of course. Then they see her big time, and laugh, and roll their eyes, and call her *Spaz*aman.

But why focus on the negatives?

Yasaman's mission: find out what that new girl, V, is telling Milla. Milla has been a mess ever since she got to school today, and now she and V are having a powwow in the somewhat-hidden nook by the water fountain. From the hall, Yasaman has a clear bead on them. Milla is wearing an insanely un-Milla shirt—it's too big for her, and it's the opposite of cute—and her normally perfect hair is draggy-saggy. V is gnawing on her lip. Not Milla's. Her own.

They're whispering back and forth. Whisper, whisper, whisper.

It better not be more lies about Katie-Rose, Yasaman thinks. Katie-Rose tried to tell Milla the truth about Tally the Turtle—there was indeed incriminating evidence on the presentation-day video, most excellent incriminating evidence that showed *Modessa with the turtle*—but so far, Milla's been ignoring her. And now Milla's out here with V, who's rapidly becoming one of the Populars and thus isn't to be trusted.

Anyway, why aren't Milla and V in class? Shouldn't they be in class?

Yasaman has a legitimate reason to be roaming the halls, because Ms. Perez asked her to go get crackers for morning snack.

But Yasaman would bet a solid-gold lira that V and Milla are illegitimately roaming the halls. Or, not roaming. *Fake* roaming—or rather, fake *un*-roaming, since they're sitting on their bums. They are illegitimately fake un-roaming, and they probably told Mr. Emerson they had some very important need to take care of, like lancing a wart or getting a Band-Aid. Or possibly getting a snack a for Mr. Emerson's class, although *no snack is being gotten*.

Ex*treme*ly suspicious. Yasaman fears that V is planting more lies in Milla's head, so that even when the truth comes out, Milla won't be able to hear it. That can happen. Yasaman's seen it on the Turkish soap operas her mother loves so much. A person can get so trapped in her cramped and unhappy vision of the world that she no longer sees the sun shining through the clouds.

Yasaman meanders—*la la la*—closer to the water fountain. The snack cabinets are on the opposite wall, and Yasaman pretends to think very very hard about just which cabinet she will open. Will it be the one labeled PAPER GOODS? Or will it be the intriguing SPARE CLOTHES cabinet? That's where they keep donated hand-me-down underwear for preschoolers who have bathroom accidents. The undies have RIVENDELL written in permanent marker on the elastic bands, just in case any preschooler is tempted to hang on to them forever as a keepsake.

Nigar had a bathroom accident after those boys tortured her. Nigar never has accidents—she's been potty-trained since the day she turned two—but she did yesterday. She had to bring her damp undies home in a plastic bag. They were her Dora the Explorer ones, the ones that say, "*¡Vámonos!* Let's go!"

After Yasaman gets the snack—if she ever *does* get the snack—she'll peek into the preschool room and check on Nigar. She'll make sure no meanie-butts are bothering her.

" . . . which is why I followed you, so I could tell you,"
V says to Milla.

Tell her what? Yasaman thinks.

"Tell me what?" Milla says.

There's a pocket of silence. A *loud* pocket of silence
that says, *I want to tell you something, but I'm scared.*

Does V know that Modessa planted Tally the Turtle
in Katie-Rose's backpack? Or, to go back even further,
does V know how Tally ended up in the commons in the
first place, shoved between the very sofa cushions that
Modessa always always *always* planted her bottom on
when the two fifth-grade classes got together? The way
V talked when Yasaman overheard her in the bathroom
with Modessa, it really seemed as if she knew something
about Tally. Something she wasn't saying. And V's comment about how Modessa should look for Tally again . . .
that was kinda weird, wasn't it?

And then, after that conversation, Modessa did indeed plop her bottom on that same sofa she always sat
on—and that's when things got interesting. Katie-Rose
has it on film. She also captured on film the shocking
moment of truth when Modessa fished beneath her

bottom and pulled out not a tack, not a dried-up Carmen booger, BUT A RED-AND-ORANGE BOBBLE-HEAD TURTLE.

There was no doubt that the turtle was Tally, thanks to Katie-Rose's serendipitous use of macro-something-ology, which she'd turned on to show Mr. Emerson. Thanks to that, Tally the Turtle filled practically the whole screen. Other than Tally, the only thing visible was Modessa's pale hand.

Katie-Rose practically blew a fuse last night when she called Yasaman and the two of them fumed over what they'd both seen. Katie-Rose could hardly form words, much less sentences. And now, by the water fountain, V seems to be having the same problem. Yasaman is now convinced that V is somehow part of this whole Tally mess.

"Violet . . . tell me what?" Milla says.

Violet, Yasaman thinks. *So that's what the V stands for.*

She'd like to turn around and get a look at Violet's face, because faces say so much more than words. Instead, she reaches up and opens the cabinet labeled SNACKS. Milla and Violet don't seem to notice that Yasaman is loitering so near them—or maybe they simply don't care?—but

Yasaman figures she'd better play it safe. She pulls down a jumbo box of Cheese Nips. She pretends to study the mile-long list of ingredients, most of which she can't pronounce.

"You had a bad day yesterday," Violet states.

"Y-y-yeah," Milla says. "But ... it got better."

"Did it? You don't *seem* better."

"Well, I am. I got Tally back, didn't I?"

Violet grunts. She must find Milla's doggedness as unconvincing as Yasaman does.

"Um, about that ...," Violet says.

Milla waits. Yasaman reads ingredients—*partially hydrogenated cottonseed and/or soybean oil? in Cheese Nips? gross!*—while keeping her ears tuned as tightly toward Violet and Milla as she can.

Violet blows air out between her lips. "There's something you should know. I haven't told anybody else. But you should know ... because, well ..."

Because you know Katie-Rose was set up, that's why! Yasaman thinks.

"Because why?" Milla asks.

"I don't know," Violet says miserably.

Yes, you do, Yasaman thinks.

"Hey," Milla says, the way a mom would to a worried child. "Hey, it's all right, Violet. You're my flower friend, remember? Flowers can tell each other things."

Yasaman holds the Cheese Nips close to her chest. *Flower friends?* she thinks. *What is Milla talking about?*

She puzzles over it, and then in a flash, she understands.

A violet is a flower.

A camilla is also a flower. Sometimes it's spelled *camellia*, or *kamilah*, which is Turkish for "perfect." But it's a flower all right. Yasaman's mom paints A LOT of flower pictures, so she knows.

And Violet and Camilla almost certainly don't know it, but Yasaman is a flower, too.

Violet breathes out. "Okay," she says to Milla. "Well, what I want to tell you ..."

Keep going, Yasaman thinks.

"... is that I have bad days, too. Almost *all* my days are bad days. I've just ... I've learned the art of crying silently, that's all."

Yasaman is as still as the cabinets in front of her, because this is *not* the confession she expected.

Milla must be equally surprised, because she says, "Oh, Violet. *Why?*"

Violet lowers her voice. Yasaman makes out the word *Mom*, and *California Regional something-or-other*, and *manic-depressed*. Or *depressive*? Something.

Violet's other words float back to her: *the art of crying silently.*

"Violet . . . ," Milla says tentatively. "You could tell the other girls, you know," Milla says. "Like Modessa and Quin. They'd understand."

No, they wouldn't, Yasaman says to herself.

Violet either nods or shakes her head, Yasaman doesn't know which. Or maybe neither. Maybe she's silently crying.

If so, she's *really* good at it, because Violet's next statement comes out like a fresh coat of brightly colored paint. "Anyway, it's all good, you know? I just . . . I didn't want you thinking . . ."

"Thanks," Milla says softly.

There are shuffling getting-up-from-the-floor sounds, and Yasaman is startled, because she forgot where she was for a second. She forgot she was eavesdropping, and in her state of shock, the jumbo box of Cheese Nips slips from her hands. Cheese Nips skitter everywhere.

Nice, Spazaman, Yasaman hears in her head. Her cheeks grow hot as she faces Milla and Violet.

"Oh *no*," Milla says, taking in the sea of tiny square crackers. She gets to her feet. "Um, let me help. Or . . . I should get a broom?"

She leaps over the expanse of Cheese Nips as best she can, but still crunches half a dozen beneath her sneaker when she lands.

"Crud," she says, glancing down. "I'll get a broom. I'll be right back!"

Milla jogs off. Now it's just Yasaman, Violet, and ten squillion Cheese Nips.

"Do you want me . . . ?" Violet starts, while at the same time Yasaman says, "You don't have to . . ."

They both stop.

"Milla's getting a broom," Yasaman says.

"Yeah, okay," Violet says. She gives a forced smile and pivots on her heel.

"Wait!" Yasaman calls.

Violet turns.

Yasaman's mouth goes dry, because she doesn't know what to say. All she knows is that she has to say *something*. She swallows. "Katie-Rose didn't steal Camilla's turtle."

Violet's eyes go wide. "I don't know what you mean."

"I mean that Katie-Rose didn't steal Tally the Turtle," Yasaman says.

"Hey, all I know is what I've heard—which is that Ms. Perez found it in Katie-Rose's backpack."

"But Katie-Rose didn't put it there."

"Well, *I* didn't put it there!"

"I know you didn't," Yasaman says. "But . . . you helped."

It's a guess, but a good one, and Yasaman knows she's hit pay dirt when Violet takes a small, maybe even unconscious step backward.

"What makes you say that?" Violet says. "How do you know?" Then, realizing she's given herself away, she wraps her arms around her ribs. She rises on her toes and looks past Yasaman, probably checking to see if Milla's on her way back yet.

"Listen," Yasaman says. "I'm not going to tell on you."

"Good, because there's nothing to tell." Violet's voice is slightly hysterical.

Yasaman bores her eyes into Violet's. "Just . . . make it right."

Violet shifts her weight. She looks away first.

"Don't let Katie-Rose take the blame," Yasaman adds.

Footsteps sound from far away. It's Milla.

"Mr. Emerson was like, 'Was there a natural disaster?'" she calls from the end of the hall. "I told him, 'Pretty much!'"

Violet smiles. To Yasaman she looks like a beautiful, fragile icicle that is so so close to shattering. There's the sense of the two of them hovering in an unfinished moment, but Milla is seconds away, and Yasaman isn't going to drag Milla into this. Modessa has dragged Milla into enough.

There is one thing, though. Yasaman steps close to Violet, who startles, and puts her hand on Violet's arm. "I'm a flower, too," she whispers. "Like you and Camilla."

Violet's eyebrows go up.

"My name, *Yasaman*. It's Turkish for 'jasmine.'"

"Oh," Violet says faintly.

Milla reaches them with a broom and a dustpan. Also,

she's put on her lime green sparkly scarf, the same one she's been wearing for the last couple of days. It doesn't do much to improve the hand-painted blue shirt, but it does make her look more Milla-ish.

"He said you should go on back to class," Milla says to Violet. "I told him I'd stay and help Yasaman."

"Um . . . okay," Violet says. Her gaze flies to Yasaman. *Are you really not going to tell?* she silently begs.

Silent crying, silent laughing, silent asking, Yasaman thinks. *So many silences.*

Just make it right, her eyes say back to Violet.

Violet hesitates, then gives a quick, almost imperceptible nod. As she strides away, Yasaman telepathically repeats her commandment: *Make it right.*

Thirty-three

Violet

"V, get over here," Quin says when the two fifth-grade classrooms join on the playground after lunch. The rain has stopped, but the sky is gray and the ground is slooshy. Right now, the teachers are saying the ice cream social is still on. But if it starts raining again before two o'clock, all bets are off.

"V!" Quin says again. "I'm *talking* to you!"

Violet bristles. *And guess what? I'm ignoring you,* Violet replies in her brain. *So go away.*

Quin marches over to the metal fence that surrounds

the playground, grabs Violet's arm, and says, "Modessa *needs* us. It's an emergency."

"What is?" Violet says.

"It's Milla. She isn't wearing Panda colors."

Violet mock-gasps. *Milla isn't wearing Panda colors? The horror!*

"Uh-huh," Quin says. "Now do you understand?"

Modessa is over in the preschoolers' play area. Since the preschoolers don't usually have recess at the same time as the older kids, Modessa has the spot to herself. She's wearing a snow-white shrug over a snow-white tank top, and Violet thinks how awesome it would be if someone just happened to pour a bucket of mud over her.

Modessa nods curtly when she sees Violet. "Good. We need to strategize."

"What's the problem?" Violet says. She wants out of Quin and Modessa's clique, but she's not sure how one does such a thing without drama and complicated-ness, which she has had enough of already. "So Milla isn't wearing Panda colors. Who cares?"

Modessa presses her lips together. "*I* do."

"Me, too," Quin chimes in.

"A, the shirt she's wearing is hideous," Modessa says, ticking points off on her fingers. "B, she's not giving Katie-Rose the cold shoulder like she's supposed to—"

"Yeah," Quin interrupts. "She's not being friendly toward her, but she's not being unfriendly, either. She's being *nothing.*"

Modessa glares at Quin. "And *C,* she's not acting appropriately thankful for everything I've done for her."

Violet has gotten caught up in Modessa's fingernails instead of her arguments. They're pink and pearly and don't fit with the gloom of the day. Black would be a better fit for Modessa, or deep dark purple. Deep dark purple would be much more fitting for a Gorgon.

Violet smiles bitterly.

"She's laughing," Quin accuses. "Modessa, V is *not* taking this seriously."

"Taking what seriously?" Violet says. She glances from Quin's face to Modessa's and remembers. "Oh. Bad Panda. *Right.*"

Her thoughts dart to Katie-Rose, and what Yasaman said about not letting her take the blame for stealing Tally. Guilt splashes over her, and she decides it's time. Time to wash her hands of these girls, and if it leads to drama, it leads to drama. Strangely, that shift to acceptance makes her stand a little taller

"I think you're overreacting, Modessa," she says.

Quin sucks in her breath. She honestly does, and it makes a spitty sound as it passes over her teeth.

Modessa regards Violet in a way that makes Violet nervous. "And I think you're underreacting."

"Well, I'm not," Violet says. It's not much as far as comebacks go, but it's something.

"I think you've lost sight of what's important," Modessa goes on. Her voice is dangerous, and even though Violet wants out—she does, she wants out—it's impossible not to dread the process. Modessa's not dumb, and her meanness tells her things sometimes that others might not pick up on. "In fact, I'm beginning to wonder if you've been fooling us this whole time."

"Um, okay," Violet says. "You got me. Bye."

She turns to leave, but Modessa's next words stop her cold.

"Like, wasn't it funny how you told me to look for Tally . . . and then there Tally was?" Modessa says.

Violet swallows. She doesn't face her. "It was . . . lucky, if that's what you mean."

"I'm going to call Milla over," Modessa goes on. "I bet she'd think it was lucky, too. How you and me talked about Tally, and not five minutes later Tally shows up?"

You and I, Violet thinks, because her mom's love of language extends to proper grammar. *How you and I talked about Tally, you jerk.* But her heart is beating hard, because if Modessa tells Milla that Violet had Tally all along, or knew where Tally was, or whatever Modessa decides to say based on the slight clues she has . . .

Milla will cry again. Milla won't let Violet explain. Milla will *hate* Violet—it could happen—and Violet doesn't want to be hated. She wants to be loved.

"Modessa, don't tell Milla," Violet says, using every bit of control she has to try and keep her voice level.

Modessa laughs, and Violet closes her eyes. She sealed her fate by letting Modessa know she cares.

"Here's a thought," Modessa says, and she's done one of her head-spinning reversals, because now she's buddy-buddy peaches and cream. "I'll call Milla over—it'll be fun. And when she comes, I want you to take her scarf and throw it on the ground. Since it's not Panda colors."

Violet turns around. "What? *No*."

"Milla! Could you come here, please?"

Milla glances up from her Wordly Wise assignment, which Violet knows she didn't finish before lunch. Too much Cheese Nip clean-up to do. Milla closes her workbook, leaves it on the concrete steps, and gets to her feet. She smiles at Violet and waves.

"Aw, she likes you," Modessa says.

Violet's gut clenches. "Why are you so worried about whether she bows down to you or not?"

"I'm not worried," Modessa says. "But I rescued Tally the Turtle for her, and if she were a good friend, she'd be grateful." She cocks her head. "She should be grateful to you, too, right? For sharing your . . . funny luck?"

She says it so innocently, like a little baby, a little blonde baby, only her hair is actually a mass of writhing snakes. And they will strike.

"I wondered if it was you who planted Tally in the

sofa cushions," Modessa says, examining one of her pearly nails. She lifts her head and flashes Violet a brilliant smile. "Thanks."

Panic mounts in Violet's chest. Milla's stride has a bounce in it as she approaches.

"Why'd you wait so long, though?" Modessa says. "I mean, if you had that stupid turtle all along . . . ?"

"V had Tally?" Quin says. She turns to Violet. "You had Tally? I didn't know that. All along you were the one who stole her?"

Violet is sunk. She doesn't even bother to correct her.

"It's an *it*, Quin," Modessa says, her pleasant tone falling away. "Not a 'her.' It's a stupid, cheap, ugly toy turtle."

Quin's eyes dart back and forth between Modessa and V. It's clear she doesn't know what she's walked into.

"Hey, guys," Milla says. She seems lighter than she did this morning, when she arrived at school a wet, miserable rat. "What's up?"

Nobody speaks. Violet *should* speak, she should jump in and take charge, but her heart's thumping so hard she feels woozy.

Milla smiles, confused. "Guys?"

"Violet?" Modessa says pointedly. She lifts her brows and looks hard at Milla's scarf.

Violet sets her jaw. She shakes her head, *no*.

Modessa stops playing. She lets her meanness blaze from her eyes, and she *would* turn Violet to stone if she had the power. Instead, she does the next best thing.

"Camilla, V isn't doing very well with her training," she says coldly.

Milla wrinkles her forehead.

Quin takes her cell phone from her back pocket and snaps pictures of both of them.

"Quin, would you please take over for V, since V is being stubborn?" Modessa says.

"Huh?" Quin says.

"Stop it, Modessa," Violet says. She's more trembly than she'd like. "Stop being so awful."

Modessa ignores her. "What we *talked* about. Concerning Camilla."

"*Ohhh*," Quin says. She glances at Milla, then at Milla's scarf. "Why me?"

"Milla, you shouldn't be here," Violet says. She goes to her and tries to lead her away.

"Violet, what's going on?" Milla says.

"Do it, Quin," Modessa commands. "Now."

Quin snaps into action, stepping forward and yanking Milla's green scarf. The silky fabric tightens against Milla's neck as Quin jerks it free, and Milla stumbles. If Violet wasn't holding on to her, she'd fall.

"*Ow!*" she cries.

Violet stops, turns, and faces off with Quin. "Give it back," she demands.

Instead, Quin flings Milla's scarf as far as she can. It lands in a mud puddle by a plastic dump truck.

"Quin!" Milla says. She's on the verge of tears, which is just what Violet didn't want, and it fills Violet with shame. "Why . . . why did you do that?"

"I don't know, 'cause I felt like it," Quin says. She snaps a picture of the now-drenched scarf.

Violet is so pissed. She marches over to retrieve the scarf. The fringy bits, when she picks it up, look like seaweed. She hears Milla saying, "But my mom gave it to me. It's special."

"Then you shouldn't have brought it to school," Modessa says. "Why *did* you?"

"Because I wasn't expecting anyone to take it and throw it on the ground!"

"Well, expect the worst," Modessa says. "Come on, *Quin.*"

The two of them strut away from the preschool area, and Violet feels a massive inward collapse of relief, because though it wasn't nice what Modessa did, or what Quin did, things could have gone worse.

But then Modessa pauses, tossing words over her shoulder like poisoned breadcrumbs. "Oh, and Milla?"

Crud, Violet thinks.

"A little bird told me Katie-Rose didn't steal Tally the Turtle after all."

Milla is dazed. "Huh?"

Violet has an urgent and painful need to get to the bathroom.

"That same little bird told me something else, too," Modessa continues in a singsong. "She said *she's* the one who stole it. *The little bird stole it herself*—isn't that so sad?"

"What little bird?" Milla says.

"Don't," Violet begs.

"I'll give you a hint," Modessa says. "The little birdy's

name rhymes with … hmm. Her name rhymes with *A, B, C, D* … wanna*be*."

Modessa laughs. Quin does, too, and snaps one last picture. As for Milla, she's baffled and fragile and reminds Violet far too much of her mom during the horrible months before she was put in California's finest mental hospital.

"She means me," Violet confesses miserably. "The little bird was me."

Thirty-four

Katie-Rose's heart is a sparrow in her ribcage. Yasaman said everything would be better today, once Milla knew the truth. But Milla won't *listen* to the truth! She won't listen to Katie-Rose, period. Won't even look at her. It's like Milla's pretending Katie-Rose doesn't even exist.

It makes Katie-Rose understand the power of the silent treatment.

It's torture. *It cannot go on.*

Mr. Emerson blows the whistle to signify that it's time for everyone to come in, and kids from both fifth-grade classes meander toward the building. Katie-Rose sees Milla off by the preschool play area with Modessa, Quin, and the new girl, and decides she'll stand right here by the door and *force* Milla to acknowledge her existence.

Except if Milla spots her, she'll find a way to avoid her. So maybe she'll scoot to the side of the door and hide behind the handicapped access ramp? Yes, good idea. That way Milla won't see her until it's too late. And if Milla thinks she's a stalker, well, let her. Anything's better than being invisible.

FADE IN TO KATIE-ROSE'S FANTASY SEQUENCE:

ESTABLISHING SHOT—PLAYGROUND—END OF MORNING BREAK

Katie-Rose waits nervously behind the handicap access ramp. Anyone can see she's a good person, a nice person, and definitely not someone who would steal a bobble-head turtle.

From the playground, Milla approaches. Katie-Rose

pops out from her hiding place, and Milla draws up short, her face muscles doing that skittery thing that signifies imminent shut-down mode. Katie-Rose knows she has to act NOW.

KATIE-ROSE

Milla! Please listen. Please please please please please!

Milla tries to brush past her, but Katie-Rose doesn't let her.

KATIE-ROSE (CONT'D)

I didn't steal Tally the Turtle. I was framed!

Emotions move across Milla's face: first confusion, then gladness, then terrible, terrible remorse for assuming the worst about Katie-Rose.

MILLA

Oh, Katie-Rose! You mean it *wasn't* you?!

KATIE-ROSE

It wasn't me. Please say you believe me.

Katie-Rose tries to be brave. She tries not to show how much she has suffered.

KATIE-ROSE (CONT'D)

(in a trembling voice)

Do you believe me?

Tears shine in Milla's eyes. Tears of joy.

MILLA

Of course, Katie-Rose! I never thought you were a thief, not really!

The two girls embrace.

MILLA (CONT'D)

I'm so sorry for what I put you through!

No, *I'm* sorry! Are we . . . are we friends again?

For*ever*. We'll be friends *forever*.

FADE TO BLACK.

Only, it doesn't play out *quite* that way, because real life never does. What actually happens is this:

"Milla?" Katie-Rose says when Milla is five feet away. She steps out from behind the handicapped access ramp.

"Katie-Rose!" Milla says. "Omigosh—I'm so glad to see you!"

"Uh . . . you are?" Katie-Rose takes in Milla's mud-splattered scarf, which is balled up in Milla's hand. Then she takes in Milla's expression, which is alert and present and not glazed over at all. It's even somewhat . . . *burning*, Milla's expression.

Finally, Katie-Rose takes in the new girl's presence. V is standing anxiously by Milla and gnawing her lip. Her own, not Milla's.

Katie-Rose turns back to Milla. "You aren't mad at me anymore?"

"*No!*" Milla says. But she sure sounds mad.

"Um . . . well . . ." Katie-Rose glances up at V, who's at least half a foot taller than Katie-Rose. "Are *you* mad at me, V?"

"Violet," V says.

"Violent?!"

"*Violet*," Milla says. "She goes by Violet, not V, and no, she's not mad at you."

Katie-Rose glances from Milla to Violet and back again. "I'm confused."

Milla nods, like yes, confusion is something she's familiar with. "I'll explain during access time."

"You will?" Katie-Rose says. Access time is when the fifth graders do their small-group math, or get together with their novel study groups, or just basically tackle whatever needs to be tackled on their road to academic glory.

"Tell Ms. Perez you have to go to the media center to research something on the internet," Milla says.

"Why?" Katie-Rose says.

Mr. Emerson appears beside them. "Let's go, girls,"

he says. "Time to head in." He's handsome in his white button-down, even with the left sleeve sewn up below the elbow.

"Sorry, Mr. Emerson," Milla says. She pulls Katie-Rose into the building, and V follows along. *No, not V*, Katie-Rose self-corrects. *Violet.*

"Just claim a computer," Milla says. "Any computer. And tell Yasaman to do the same thing."

"Yasaman?" Katie-Rose says.

"She's part of this, too," Violet says.

"Part of *what*?"

"We need to all get on that site she made," Milla says. "So we can chat, and it'll be private, and no one can listen in."

"BlahBlahSomethingSomething.com," Katie-Rose says in a daze. "It . . . it needs a better name."

Violet makes a face, like *Boy, does it.*

"Once the four of us are online, we'll figure out a plan," Milla says. They reach Ms. Perez's room.

"I'm still confused," Katie-Rose says. "In fact, I'm even more confused."

Milla glances around, then speaks quickly and secretively. "Listen. I know you didn't steal Tally the Turtle. I know you were set up, *and* I know who did it."

"You do?" Katie-Rose says.

"It was Modessa," Violet says. "But ... I played a role in it, too." She blinks. "Um. My bad."

Is this really happening? Katie-Rose wonders. Her stomach is flipping around so much that she farts—but it's a silent one, and she doesn't think anyone notices.

"And then Quin threw my scarf in the mud for no good reason," Milla says. "And it's just ..." She throws her hands up. "It's got to end, that's all."

"Hence the plan," Violet says. "The top-secret, totally private, time-sensitive plan."

Katie-Rose nods excitedly. She's twisty, but it's a good twisty. A *fabulous* twisty, even if not much of what they've told her has truly sunk in.

"Okay, then," Milla says. "Talk to you soon."

Wow, Katie-Rose thinks as Camilla and Violet hurry to Mr. Emerson's room. Sometimes life is even better than a movie.

Thirty-five

The Chatterbox

The Chatterbox

MarshMilla has entered the room.

The*rose*knows has entered the room.

The*rose*knows: milla! hi!!!!! i ran to get here. +waves at
milla+

The*rose*knows: where's everyone else?

MarshMilla: violet shld be logging on soon—i gave her
the addy

The*rose*knows: i told yasaman, but where is she?

Yasaman has entered the room.

Yasaman: here i am! hi, milla! hi, k-r! omigosh,

	this is so fun to be chatting with y'all AT SCHOOL!
The*rose*knows:	i know! you should know i'm trying to compress a spazz. must . . . hold . . . in . . .
The*rose*knows:	***explodes* i luv being here with you guys!!!! i luv it oodles and bunches and bunches and oodles! bunches and bunches of LUV!**
Yasaman:	i luv it 2
The*rose*knows:	+sighs happily+ i feel so much better than i did this morning. it's like the yucky stuff going on almost doesn't even matter!!!!
MarshMilla:	oh, it matters 😟
Yasaman:	**the yucky stuff having to do with tally the turtle, u mean?**
MarshMilla:	YES. the Fake Incident of the Stolen Turtle, i shall call it. FIST for short, cuz it makes me want to punch my fist right into modessa!!!

ultraviolet has entered the room.

The*rose*knows:	medusa and her evil harpy quin, u mean

ultraviolet:	ha, that's good
ultraviolet:	hi guys
MarshMilla:	violet! hi!
ultraviolet:	so what's been covered?
Yasaman:	well . . .
ultraviolet:	wait, no. before we even go there, i need to say *sorry*
MarshMilla:	violet, u already did. water under the bridge, 'kay?
MarshMilla:	anyway, u got sucked in against yr will. how cld u have known how mean modessa is?
The*rose*knows:	um . . . how cld she NOT, milla? and for that matter, how cld *U* not know how mean medusa is?!!!
Yasaman:	she's kind of got a point
Yasaman:	is that rude? i don't mean to be rude. it's just . . . camilla, ur A LOT nicer than modessa or quin.
ultraviolet:	i agree
ultraviolet:	and milla, i already told u how sorry i am . . . but i haven't told katie-rose.
The*rose*knows:	huh?

ultraviolet: 🙁

The*rose*knows: no, seriously. sorry about what? and why the frowny face? am i missing something?

ultraviolet: no! i just wanted to apologize personally and to yr face. even tho we're, um, on computers.

The*rose*knows: ohhhh. did u already know about modessa finding tally, and you didn't say anything? cuz yasaman and i didn't figure it out until yesterday, when we really looked close at the footage i took

ultraviolet: did u, um, see anything else? on yr vid?

The*rose*knows: i saw chance dressed up like an olive. not a great look for him.

ultraviolet: katie-rose, i put tally there. i stuck talley b/w the sofa cushions. and that's what i'm apolgizing for. i wanted modessa to find her, but only cuz i thought she'd give her back to milla. i swear.

The*rose*knows: but . . . huh? how did *u* come to have talley?

Yasaman: wait u had her from the beginning, didn't u, violet? omigosh, u had her all along.

ultraviolet:	well, yeah . . . but i thought u knew that already. yr whole "make it right" speech?
Yasaman:	i knew *something* was going on. i overheard u & modessa talking in the bathroom. that's why u told modessa to look harder? and then u ran out and put tally where u knew she'd sit?
ultraviolet:	y-y-y-y-yeah
The*rose*knows:	u had tally the whole time?! ever since monday, when milla first "lost" her?
ultraviolet:	hold on. why r u saying it like that? i didn't *steal* tally, katie-rose.
MarshMilla:	guys . . . let's not fight, plz? hasn't there been enuff fighting?
The*rose*knows:	u could have cleared my name right away, when modessa said i stole tally the turtle.
ultraviolet:	i know. but . . . i didn't
MarshMilla:	she's super-sorry, tho, katie-rose. she explained the whole story to me during break. and i'm sorry 2, for believing what modessa said. i shld have known better.

ultraviolet:	i AM sorry, katie-rose. I feel terrible
ultraviolet:	um, k-r?
ultraviolet:	u've gone quiet on me. like, radio silence quiet, ALL of u
ultraviolet:	u hate me, don't u?
Yasaman:	no, of course not. i was just giving katie-rose a chance to respond.
Yasaman:	katie-rose?
ultraviolet:	she's had a chance to respond. she's not responding.
MarshMilla:	did she leave?
Yasaman:	i don't think so. if she logged out, a message bubble wld pop up and say so
ultraviolet:	great, this is just great
ultraviolet:	i suck, basically
Yasaman:	katie-rose, say something!
MarshMilla:	violet, do u think . . . maybe . . . u shld tell her about . . . u know? yr own bad days and all that?
ultraviolet:	uh, NO
ultraviolet:	i don't even know what ur talking about

Yasaman:	about violet's mom? is that what u mean, milla?
MarshMilla:	yasaman—how do u know about that?!
Yasaman:	cuz violet, it's not anything to be ashamed of.
Yasaman:	and i kinda overheard u in the hall this morning, before the cheese nip explosion.
MarshMilla:	wow. u overhear a lot
Yasaman:	um, it's kinda 1 of my talents
ultraviolet:	okaaaaaay, well, i think i'm gonna go
Yasaman:	plz don't! i shouldn't have mentioned yr mom. i should have kept my mouth shut.
ultraviolet:	yeah, whatev. it's been real. bye.
The*rose*knows:	no, violet, stay
Yasaman:	katie-rose!!!! we worried u'd logged off!
MarshMilla:	yeah, u shldn't disappear on us like that!
The*rose*knows:	u guys, let me say something
The*rose*knows:	violet—u still here?
ultraviolet:	still here
The*rose*knows:	ok. +big breath+
The*rose*knows:	violet, whatever's going on with u and yr mom . . . u don't have to tell

me. i mean, u can if u want to, but . . .
whatever.

The*rose*knows: and about what u did . . . well, i guess i
was so busy worrying about milla being
mad at me that when it turned out she
wasn't, all i felt was GLAD.

The*rose*knows: but just now, when u said how u cld have
spoken up earlier . . .

The*rose*knows: it made me feel bad all over again

ultraviolet: which is why i apologized

The*rose*knows: yeah. i get that. +straightens spine+

The*rose*knows: thank u. um, apology accepted

Yasaman: i think it was wrong what u did, violet . . .
but brave of u to apologize. lots of ppl don't
ever apologize.

MarshMilla: yeah. lots of ppl do worse things and
don't even CARE that they hurt ppl.

ultraviolet: Medusa and her evil harpy Quin?

MarshMilla: yup, and that's why i wanted to talk to
you guys. i think we should—

MarshMilla: wait. start over. i think THEY—and by
"they" of course i mean medusa and

quin—should experience what it feels like to be on the other side of the stick, or whatever the expression is.

The*rose*knows: i agree, 100%

ultraviolet: so what do we do?

Yasaman: only . . . quick insert . . . it won't involve doing something bad to them, will it?

Yasaman: violence is against my religion.

MarshMilla: +taps chin+ what if we made them THINK we did something bad . . . but we don't actually **do** the bad thing?

The*rose*knows:

ultraviolet: yeah, what she said

Yasaman: who, milla or katie-rose?

ultraviolet: both

ultraviolet:

The*rose*knows: milla? explain

MarshMilla: it has to do with something max told me

The*rose*knows: max? as in, MAX max?

MarshMilla: max-max, that's cute. we shld call him that!

The*rose*knows: speaking of . . . milla, is that max's shirt ur wearing?!

MarshMilla:	yes, cuz he was a gentleman and let me borrow it. cuz mine got wet. and we talked about rain . . . and windshield wipers . . . and how things aren't always the way u think they are.
The*rose*knows:	**max** said all that?
MarshMilla:	maybe not in those exact words, but yeah.
MarshMilla:	anyway, it made me remember the time quin put mud in my chocolate milkshake.
Yasaman:	quin put . . . ? WHY?
ultraviolet:	typical 😝
The*rose*knows:	why did talking about windshield wipers make u think about *that*?
MarshMilla:	cuz my milkshake wasn't a milkshake. it was a *mudshake*
MarshMilla:	and quin and modessa aren't what i thought they were, either. now OR then
The*Rose*Knows:	ohhhhhh
The*rose*knows:	but i still don't know where ur going with this
Yasaman:	me neither 😐
MarshMilla:	well, we're having the ice cream social at

2, right? and there's an awful lot of mud
on the playground . . . and mud looks a lot
like chocolate syrup . . .

Yasaman:

The*rose*knows: yeah. huh???

MarshMilla: i'll spell it out. modessa and quin play
dirty, can we all agree on that?

The*rose*knows: literally!

MarshMilla: add in some lying (them), confusion (us),
and crying (me), and you get a perfect
friend-tastrophe. only, the friends i'm
talking about aren't modessa and quin. i
am *over* that train to nowhere.

The*rose*knows: are we the friends ur talking about? me
and yasaman and violet?

MarshMilla: yes, u and yasaman and violet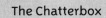

MarshMilla: we might have to make up a flower name
for yasaman, tho. just to match the rest
of us.

ultraviolet: actually, no u won't

ultraviolet: yasaman, tell them what yr name means in
turkish

Yasaman:	it means "jasmine." so i already AM a flower, just like you all 😊
MarshMilla:	no way!
The*rose*knows:	yasaman = jasmine? **cool!**
The*rose*knows:	but milla, how r *U* a flower?
MarshMilla:	cuz a camilla IS my mom abigail's favorite kind of flower. that's why they named me that.
The*rose*knows:	ohhh! i think im gonna cry!!! 😢
MarshMilla:	don't cry, silly
The*rose*knows:	but we're all flowers!!!! it's like . . . FATE!
The*rose*knows:	and flowers grow in the dirt! and need rain! which turns the dirt into mud! and i have no idea why i'm saying this except that i am!
Yasaman:	**will someone plz tell me what the friend-tastrophe has to do with mud and the ice cream social? cuz i don't wanna mess up!**
MarshMilla:	here's what i'm thinking. we plant the *idea* that maybe, just maybe, quin put mud in modessa's ice cream sundae . . . and we c what happens. cuz if modessa

is small-minded enuff to think quin really wld do something like that—

The*rose*knows: which she WLD, as u know from personal experience!

MarshMilla: well, so *ha ha* to them if they fall for it. it wld be . . .

MarshMilla: ack. there's a term for what i'm talking about, we learned it last year. like in the lion king, when scar kills mufasa by pushing him over the edge of a cliff, and then scar ends up dying the exact same way?

The*rose*knows: it's when the villain gets what he deserves. i can't remember what it's called.

ultraviolet: poetic justice?

MarshMilla: poetic justice! right!

The*rose*knows: well, i for one am **all about** poetic-justicing modessa and quin!

Yasaman: me 2

MarshMilla: let's get to it, then. we've only got fifteen minutes to nail down our plan . . .

The*rose*knows: flowers for justice! yay! ✿ ✿ ✿ ✿

1:55: Ms. Perez tells her class to line up by the back door of the room to go to the ice cream social, the door that leads straight out to the playground. Milla *should* be with her class in Mr. Emerson's room, but she wants to see the first part of the plan put into action with her very own eyes. So she's peeking sneakily in from the hall.

And *eeee*, it's happening!!! Katie-Rose goes up to Ms. Perez and says, "Ms. Perez, Quin has her cell phone in her pocket."

Ms. Perez makes a pained face and strides to where Quin stands. "Cell phone, Quin," she says. "Hand it over."

Quin's jaw drops. "I'm not doing anything! Ms. P*erez*!"

"You know the rules. Cell phones stay in your cubby."

Pouting, Quin pulls her celly out of her back pocket and hands it over. Milla bets Quin wants to say, "Modessa has hers, too," but amazingly, she doesn't.

Ms. Perez puts Quin's phone in Quin's cubby. "Next time I'm keeping it and calling your parents. Now. Are we ready to go outside?"

"Yes ma'am," Katie-Rose and Yasaman chorus with the rest of the students. Milla grins and dashes back to her own class, squeezing in near the front of the line.

. . . .

2:00: Milla, Katie-Rose, Yasaman, and Violet are among the first to reach the playground. There is much hyper giggling, especially by Katie-Rose. Milla doesn't mind. She decides it's more important to have fun and be silly than to worry about looking dumb by having fun and being silly. She also knots Max's shirt at belly button level and fantasizes briefly about starting a geektastic fashion trend. Then she laughs at herself, realizing that she still cares about appearances despite herself. She probably always will.

· · · ·

2:01: Yasaman grabs Milla's arm. "Here they come," she says. Milla's heart flops as Modessa and Quin stroll from the building.

"Hi, girls," Milla calls.

"Er . . . hi, Milla," Quin says, looking confused that Milla's speaking to them.

Modessa snorts, and Quin changes her expression. She snorts, too.

· · · ·

2:02: Katie-Rose says fakily, "Let's go get some ice cream!"

"Yes, let's!" Violet replies, equally chirpy. The "chirpy" is to tease Katie-Rose, but in a nice way, not a mean one.

The four flowers walk in flanked formation to the ice cream tables set up by parent volunteers. If they were in a movie, theme-song music would swell majestically.

· · · ·

2:03: Violet drizzles Hershey's Syrup into a Styrofoam bowl. No ice cream, just Hershey's Syrup.

"Oh, doll, you're not eating just that, are you?" asks one of the mothers who's helping out. She raises her eyebrows in a mom-scolding way, and Milla wonders if

Violet feels a pang for her own mom, who isn't around to scold Violet even if all Violet *did* eat was Hershey's Syrup.

"Yep," Violet says smoothly to the woman.

That Violet, she's one cool customer, Milla thinks.

. . . .

2:04: On the other side of the table, Modessa dumps the entire container of mini M&M's onto her ice cream. It's so typical of her not to leave any for anyone else. Yasaman moves into position as Modessa continues down the serving table. As Modessa sticks her spoon into the jar of cherries, Yasaman stumbles into her.

"Watch it, *Spaz*aman!" Modessa says sharply, even though it was just a little bump, not even big enough to make Modessa drop the cherry.

"Sorry, sorry," Yasaman says, and Modessa exhales loudly.

. . . .

Also at 2:04: While Yasaman distracts Modessa, Katie-Rose says (again, fakily), "Oh no! Some preschoolers have Quin's cell phone!"

But even though her delivery is wooden, and even though Quin should know her cell phone is safe in her cubby, Quin falls for it. Just the thought of harm coming to her precious celly throws her into a tizzy.

"What'd you say?" she cries, whipping her head around. "Who? Where?"

"There!" Katie-Rose, gesturing at the two boys who, according to Yasaman, were mean to Yasaman's sister, Nigar. The preschoolers aren't normally outside with the older kids, but today they are because of the ice cream social.

"Oh, nuh-*uh*," Quin says, striding angrily toward the boys.

· · · ·

2:05–2:07: Milla approaches Modessa and says, "You shouldn't be mean to people. If you keep being mean to people, you won't have any friends."

"Ex*cuse* me?" Modessa says. When she turns to Milla in disbelief, Yasaman is in a perfect position to swipe Modessa's sundae, which she does. She fast-walks off with it, Katie-Rose joining her and giggling madly.

"Like how you were mean to Yasaman just now," Milla says, staying focused. "And how you told Quin to throw my scarf in the mud."

Modessa makes a scornful *chhh* sound. "What*ev*er."

"Some day Quin is going to get sick of taking your

orders," Milla continues. "Some day she's going to be done with you, just like I am."

"Oh, please. You're 'done' with me? For today, maybe. You'll come running back on Monday."

Milla shakes her head. This time she won't.

Modessa must see something of this in Milla's expression, because her arrogance wavers.

"Well . . . well . . . *you* might be stupid enough to think you can make it through fifth grade without me, but Quin isn't," Modessa says. "Right, Quin?" She glances around. "*Quin?!*"

. . . .

2:08: Katie-Rose and Yasaman reach the opposite side of the playground, where Ms. Perez is standing with some of the other teachers. As Katie-Rose approaches Ms. Perez, Yasaman continues to the bench the teachers use for time-outs. There, she furtively deposits Modessa's sundae. She keeps moving, circling back toward the grassy area. She gives Violet a quick nod.

. . . .

2:09: "Excuse me, Ms. Perez?" Katie-Rose says. She taps Ms. Perez's arm.

Ms. Perez turns. "Yes?"

"Quin is bullying some preschoolers," Katie-Rose says. Out of the corner of her eye, she sees Violet sauntering toward Modessa's kidnapped sundae with her bowl of Hershey's syrup.

Ms. Perez glances toward the preschool area, and her eyebrows shoot up. Quin is with two little kids, all right, but from the looks of it, Quin is barely holding her own.

"Poopy-head!" one of them yells, stomping on Quin's foot.

The other sticks out his tongue and taunts, "Ta-duh, ta-duh, *ta*-duh!" Which makes no sense, but he's a preschooler.

But Quin is a fifth grader, and much bigger, and anyway should know the rules about intimidation. So when she puts her hands on her hips and steps within inches of the *ta-duh, ta-duh* boy, Ms. Perez presses her lips together and makes a beeline for her.

· · · ·

2:10: By the looks of it, Ms. Perez is giving Quin a stern talking-to. *Ha ha*, thinks Milla when she glances over. *Serves you right for making fun of her underwear.*

She deftly rotates her body to keep Modessa from

seeing what's going on. "Told you she was going to disappear," she says.

Natalia Totenburg, who's behind them, butts into their conversation. "Who dithappeared?" she asks.

"Quin," Milla replies. "She finally had enough of Modessa."

. . . .

2:11: Yasaman catches Milla's eye and gives her a thumbs-up, which means that Katie-Rose has given the same signal to Yasaman. Which tells Milla that yes, Ms. Perez has done her job, and Quin is on her way to the time-out bench.

Milla feels a thrill at the base of her spine. She says to Modessa, "I understand why Quin ditched you. Why'd she take your ice cream, though?"

"Thee took your ithe cream?" Natalia echoes.

Modessa drops her gaze to the table. She sees that her ice cream is indeed gone, and she makes an indignant sound. The cherry balanced on her spoon tips and falls.

. . . .

2:12–2:14: Yasaman joins Milla at the ice cream table.

"*There* you are," Yasaman says breathlessly. "I saw Quin on the other side of the playground, and thought—"

316

"You saw Quin?" Modessa demands. "Where?"

Yasaman widens her eyes. The goal is to make Modessa think she just wanted to talk to Milla, and that in her hurry she didn't notice Modessa was here, too. "Um . . . um . . ."

"Where is Quin, *Spaz*aman? Tell me!"

Yasaman honestly looks nervous. She's a much better actor than Katie-Rose . . . or maybe she's not acting. She turns to Milla and says, with perfect confusion, "So . . . you're not part of what's going on?"

"What *is* going on?" Modessa says.

"Yeah, Yathaman," Natalia says. "What'th going on?"

"Well, I saw Quin . . ." Yasaman's gaze darts to Modessa, then back to Milla. Milla encourages her with a nod. "And, um, she's got someone's ice cream—"

"What do you mean, she's got someone's ice cream?" Modessa snaps.

"Modessa, don't kill the messenger," Milla says. "Sheesh." She puts her hand on Yasaman's arm. "It's okay, Yasaman."

"Yeah," Natalia says. "You can tell uhth."

Yasaman is distracted for a second by Natalia. She shakes her head and refocuses.

"It's just that I remembered what you told me, about how Quin put mud in your milkshake that one time. And I thought . . . maybe . . ." She gulps. "Never mind. I'm sure I'm wrong."

"Quin has a behavior disorder," Milla says. "At least this time she doesn't have *my* ice cream." She puts her hands on her hips. "By the way, Modessa. Did you tell Quin to do that? To put mud in my milkshake that day? 'Cause that was really uncool."

Natalia is appalled. "You put mud in Milla'th milkthake? *Tho* uncool."

Yasaman squints deliberately at the time-out bench. The other girls' gazes follow hers. "Whose ice cream did she put mud in this time?"

Milla shakes her head. "Like I said, it's not mine."

Modessa's face is grim. "It's *mine*," she says, storming toward the bench.

. . . .

2:15: Milla and Yasaman share a quick look of delight (plus a squinch of horror that their plan is actually *working*) and race after Modessa.

"Hey, where are you guyth going?" Natalia calls.

"Nowhere!" Milla shouts over her shoulder.

Katie-Rose and Violet join Milla and Yasaman just as Modessa reaches the bench.

"You stole my ice cream!" Modessa says angrily to Quin.

Quin, who's *not* a happy camper, lifts her head. "What?"

"Don't lie. It's *right there*." Modessa juts her chin at the bowl of ice cream next to Quin. In addition to its hoggish portion of mini M&M's, Modessa's sundae now has noticeably more chocolate syrup on it than it originally did. "I have *eyes*, you know."

Quin frowns at the ice cream. "That's yours? It was here when I sat down!"

"Oh, please."

"Modessa"—she's starting to freak—"I don't know anything about that ice cream. I swear!"

Modessa makes an ugly sound. "Just like you don't know *anything* about the mud you put on it? You are *so* lame, Quin."

Milla feels a hand squeezing hers. She squeezes back. Quin spots Milla and her posse and grows more flustered.

"Come on, I would *never* do something like that!" she protests.

"Yeah, uh-huh. And that's why there's so much more 'chocolate syrup'"—she makes air quotes—"on it now?" She picks up the bowl. "Since you like mud so much, *you* eat it."

. . . .

2:16: Modessa shoves the bowl at Quin's face. Quin blocks Modessa's thrust with her forearm. The bowl of ice cream flies up . . . it's moving in slow motion, arching gracefully through the air . . . flipping upside-down . . . and then, *zwoop*. Time kicks back in, and so does gravity.

Milla draws her hands to her mouth, inhaling sharply at the amount of damage one bowl of ice cream can do. Sploopy goo lands in Quin's hair. Chocolate sauce splatters Modessa's white shrug and Quin's white shirt. Miniature M&M's fleck both of them like multicolored chicken pox.

It is a moment made of awesome.

"*Ewww!*" Modessa wails, extending her arms away from her torso. "I'm all gross!"

"I'm *grosser!*" Quin whines. A glop of ice cream slides

from her hair to her collarbone and slips down her shirt. She squeals.

Violet laughs first. That gets Katie-Rose going. And once she's going, there's no stopping her. Yasaman presses her knuckles to her mouth, but there's a smile under there, Milla can tell. As for Milla herself . . .

Well, she doesn't feel scared anymore. She feels free. Full of joy, like a radiant white balloon. *No*, a sparkly green balloon.

Understanding dawns in Modessa's eyes.

"*You* did this," she says dangerously. She approaches them, and they yelp and clutch each other.

"We didn't do anything," Katie-Rose says, her voice high. She twists her head over her shoulder. "Ms. Perez! Ms. Perez, help!"

Ms. Perez is there in a nanosecond. She looks Quin and Modessa up and down and says, "Girls, what is going on? Quin, you're supposed to be taking a break. Why are you covered in ice cream?"

Modessa points a sticky finger at Milla, Katie-Rose, Yasaman, and Violet. "They put mud in my ice cream and made me think Quin did it!"

"We did not!" Milla says passionately.

Ms. Perez presses her lips together. She focuses on the most trustworthy girl in the group. "Yasaman?"

Yasaman's dark eyes convey dismay. "*No*, Ms. Perez. We would never put mud in someone's ice cream."

Modessa squats, grabs the ice cream bowl, and thrusts it at Yasaman. Modessa and Quin are wearing most of its contents, but a small amount of ice cream and chocolate sauce remain.

"Prove it," she says. "Ms. Perez, make her taste it."

Yasaman shakes her head. "Um, I'd rather not." She appeals to Ms. Perez. "What if *she* put mud in it herself? She's done it before."

Ms. Perez presses her fingertips to her brow. She briefly closes her eyes. "Girls," she says, "did *any* of you put mud in this ice cream?"

"No way," Violet says. Milla, Katie-Rose, and Yasaman shake their heads.

"*I* didn't!" Modessa says indignantly.

Ms. Perez turns to Quin. "Quin?"

"I don't even know how it *got* here!" Quin says.

Modessa makes her *oh please* grunt before remembering that she switched stories and now thinks Quin has been framed.

Just like Katie-Rose was framed, thinks Milla, experiencing a moment of guilt.

There's a difference, however. Modessa came right out and said, "Katie-Rose stole Camilla's turtle!" Milla and the others just set up the ice cream situation . . . and then let Modessa assume what she chose. And since Modessa has a small, petty heart, she assumed the worse—even of her supposed bestie.

Ms. Perez holds out her hand. All six girls glance at each other in confusion.

She wiggles her fingers. "The bowl, please?"

Warily, Modessa surrenders it.

Ms. Perez dips her finger into the chocolate sauce and puts it in her mouth. Katie-Rose's eyes pop. Ms. Perez's finger is clean when she pulls it out, and she says, "No mud. Just Hershey's Syrup." She eyes them one by one to convey her exasperation. "Do I need to send you girls to see Mrs. Westerfeld?"

Mrs. Westerfeld is Rivendell's principal. She's nice, but can be frightening when required.

"No, ma'am," Yasaman says. Milla, Violet, and Katie-Rose follow suit.

Ms. Perez turns to Quin and Modessa.

"No, ma'am," Modessa mumbles. She flicks Quin's hip.

"*Ow*," Quin says. Sullenly, she meets Ms. Perez's eyes and shakes her head.

"Then Quin and Modessa, why don't you stop acting like children and go clean yourselves up." She shifts her attention to Milla and the others. "The rest of you, just . . . do something peaceful for the rest of the hour. Can you manage that?"

There's head-nodding and *yes, ma'am*-ing, and Ms. Perez leaves.

"Good Lord, I need a new job," they hear her mutter.

Milla faces Modessa and Quin. Modessa steps forward, and Milla squares up against her. She senses Violet, Yasaman, and Katie-Rose move closer in.

"You're dead," Modessa says.

"No, I'm alive, actually," Milla says. She's amazed at how steady her voice is. "Better go clean yourselves up, don't you think?" She doesn't add "*children*" to the end of her sentence. She doesn't need to.

Modessa glares bullets, then makes a drama-queen *ummph* and flounces off. Quin's flounce is less graceful, but flouncy just the same. A dreadlock of ice-cream-y hair hangs lankily down her back.

"Bye, Medusa and her evil harpy Quin," Violet sing-songs.

Modessa's spine stiffens, but she doesn't turn around.

"*Eeee!*" Katie-Rose squeals, no longer able to contain her glee. All four girls are giddy and exhilarated and stunned, and their laughter crescendos until Yasaman says "shhh" and uses a head-tilt to indicate Ms. Perez, who's glancing at them in warning.

So they form a circle. Their faces are bright.

"Omigosh," Milla marvels. "We did it!"

"We are brill-i-ant-ay," Katie-Rose says.

"Why yes, we are," Violet says. She adopts a silly radio announcer's voice. "That's right, folks. You heard it here first: Medusa and her evil harpy Quin are trumped by a bunch of flowers."

"A lovely bunch of flowers," Milla says, flinging her arms wide and doing a spin, "which is loved bunches and bunches by me."

"Love you bunches!" Katie-Rose repeats. She bounces on her heels. "Omigosh! Love you bunches!"

She looks at Yasaman, who grins. *Yes-ness* passes between them.

"What?" Milla says. "You guys are thinking something. Tell us!"

Violet tilts her head. "I think I know," she says. "Needs a *teeny* bit of tweaking, though. Like, l-u-v love, and maybe 'luv ya' instead of 'luv you'?"

"LuvYaBunches.com," Yasaman says blissfully. "It's *perfect*."

SATURDAY, AUGUST 29

Thirty-seven

Luv Ya Bunches.com

	The FLOWER Box
Yasaman:	hi, guys! +waves at friends+
ultraviolet:	hola.
MarshMilla:	ooo, yaz, i luv the new chatroom name! the flower box instead of the chatterbox?
The*rose*knows:	vair vair clever
The*rose*knows:	and now: yay for it being saturday!!! yay for our first week of school being so fabulous!!!!
MarshMilla:	it didn't start off that way
The*rose*knows:	true dat

ultraviolet:	FO SHO
Yasaman:	**uh . . . yo yo yo?**
MarshMilla:	+stares blankly at friends+
MarshMilla:	you guys r weird
The*rose*knows:	takes 1 to know 1!
ultraviolet:	yasaman, i can't believe u said "yo yo yo."
Yasaman:	**+giggles+ i can't either. don't tell my dad**
ultraviolet:	i might. *brring brring!* "hello, mr. yasaman's father? yr daughter said *yo yo yo*"
MarshMilla:	so what's everybody going to do over the weekend?
The*rose*knows:	shoot some video, prolly
The*rose*knows:	wanna be in it? i'll make u a Star, dahlink!
MarshMilla:	wow. that looks so much like me, it's uncanny
The*rose*knows:	i *know*, right? +giggles+
ultraviolet:	don't start with yr giggling, k-r. i can't take it this early in the morning.
The*rose*knows:	wah wah wah. actually it's gonna be a video of a domino course max set up. it's got 500 dominoes AND an elusive reverse

	domino effect AND, apparently, a robot with a time delay.
The*rose*knows:	milla . . . max said *u* helped come up with that part?
MarshMilla:	me? no. no way
MarshMilla:	he said that?
The*rose*knows:	he wants me to capture it on film when he knocks them down, and i said sure, as long as he lets me post it on blahblahsomethingsomething.com.
The*rose*knows:	ag! i mean luvyabunches.com!!!! +thwonks head+. but then u can all c it, k? i think it'll be cool.
MarshMilla:	it sounds cool
Yasaman:	**what about u, violet? what r u doing today?**
ultraviolet:	well . . . i've got kind of exciting-ish (maybe) plans. i'm, uh, going to visit my mom. at the hospital.
MarshMilla:	violet! that's awesome!
ultraviolet:	i hope. or it could suck
The*rose*knows:	will u tell me about her 1 day? it doesn't have to be today . . . but 1 day?

ultraviolet:	yeah. 1 day soon
Yasaman:	i hope she's doing *great*, violet 
Yasaman:	that's me offering u luv, if u can't tell
ultraviolet:	thx
ultraviolet:	what about u, yaz? what r yr big plans?
Yasaman:	chores, chores, and more chores. then tonite we go to the mosque.
Yasaman:	however, i'm ALSO gonna find time for EMPOWERMENT LESSONS WITH NIGAR!
MarshMilla:	???
Yasaman:	well, you guys have empowered ME so much, and i want to spread the love. i want Nigar to feel like she can handle it if those mean boys say mean things to her again.
ultraviolet:	yeah! tell her to smack 'em upside the head!
Yasaman:	um, well . . .
ultraviolet:	JK! sheesh! i know ur all about peace, yaz
MarshMilla:	that's cool that ur gonna give her empowerment lessons
MarshMilla:	we might all need some, ya know?
The*rose*knows:	huh? we already *are* empowered

MarshMilla:	yes . . . but medusa and her evil harpy Quin aren't gonna fade away into the woodwork, ya know. there's gonna be round 2 to this battle. maybe even round 3 and 4 and so on, all the way to infinity.
ultraviolet:	well, we'll just have to handle it, won't we?
MarshMilla:	absotootly
Yasaman:	can i say something?
MarshMilla:	of course. it's yr site, yaz.
Yasaman:	um . . . i just hope we don't focus ONLY on medusa and her evil harpy Quin. there r other things we cld do with our super-duper flower power, ya know.
MarshMilla:	"flower power," i luv it
The*rose*knows:	what do u have in mind?
Yasaman:	well . . . don't laff . . . we cld campaign for better snacks! those cheese nips they give us? they're full of hydrogenated oils!
MarshMilla:	😮
Yasaman:	seriously, do u know how bad that stuff is?
The*rose*knows:	*i* do. it's BAD BAD BAD, peoples!

MarshMilla: um, i have an idea. we could get to know max-max better, maybe. if we felt like it.

The*rose*knows: holy fish cakes! milla, **do** u like max-max?!!

MarshMilla: NOOOOOOO! i'm just saying MAYBE we cld get to know him better. maybe!!!

Yasaman: hmmm. verrrrry interesting

ultraviolet: yaz?

Yasaman: yes, violet?

ultraviolet: what does an octopus have to do with anything?

The*rose*knows: i like the octopus! it's cute!

MarshMilla: yeah, silly violet

ultraviolet: milla? what do mushrooms . . . ?

ultraviolet: oh, nvm

Yasaman: back to next week: i don't really care what we do as long as we make it GREAT, is all.

The*rose*knows: with the bunch of us together, that's a given

MarshMilla: aw, group hug! group hug!

ultraviolet: hey, guys? i've g2g—MY dad's calling

Yasaman:	yeah, i shld go 2. 1 last thing, tho
Yasaman:	milla . . . i made this just for u: 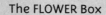
MarshMilla:	+tears up+ oh, yaz, i lub it!!!!
MarshMilla:	i lub all u guys! ♥ ♥ ♥
ultraviolet:	yeah, we're pretty fab 😉
ultraviolet:	and on that note . . . bye!
The*rose*knows:	bye! milla, call me if u wanna come vover and help me film max-max!!!!!!
MarshMilla:	ha ha
Yasaman:	farewell for now, my flower friends!!!! luv ya bunches!!!! 🌼 🌼 🌼 🌼

And that's how the seeds of our friendship were planted. Now it's up to us to let them grow.

Acknowledgments

To those who helped this novel bloom, I thank you!

From my home turf: Moran and Maysie, who gave me DIRT. Rachel, who taught me that a "camilla" is a flower. Al and Quinn, who taught me about the elusive reverse domino effect. Kazim, for talking to me about Islam and Turkey—though anything I got wrong came from me and not him! Chelsea Alles, for being a sweetie pie. Julia Meier, who rains love on me and mine and helps us lift our happy faces toward the sun.

From the turf universal: Bob, who makes the best fertilizer *on the planet*. Sarah Mlynowski, who read an early draft and told me how to make it better. All my buddies from the cookie jar and from peacelovebabyducks.ning.com, who answer my silly girly questions at the drop of a ~~hat~~ chocolate chip cookie. My big ol' honking family, always and forever.

From the land of books, where everyone is hipper than I: the entire Abrams sales team, for caring. Christine Norrie for bringing Violet, Katie-Rose, color adorableness. Chad Beckerman for embracing pinkness and turtles and ...ped like Scott Auerbach, for caring whether there are many Cyclopes or just one. Jason Wells, for being the kind of cool dude who says "YES!" to cupcakes with flowers on them. Michael Jacobs, for two-fisting it with me at fancy book events, and for supporting books in general, so that we can attend fancy book events. Barry Goldblatt for not being afraid of girls without noses. And—oh, I swoon—a special bouquet of aromatic thanks to the wonderful, amazing, brilliant, and clever Susan Van Metre, my editor, who wore her bewitching girdle every day while slaving over this baby (and thank goodness, for it made all the difference). I 🖤 U, Susan!!!!!

And from the loamy depths of my soul: Mirabelle, Jamie, Al, and Jack, for existing in this beautiful world. Without you, I would wilt, but with you, I am a dandelion bursting with joy. You are the flowers of my heart!

About the Author

Lauren Myracle *really* likes tweens and pre-tweens; she'd rather sit at the "kids' table" than at the boring grown-up table any day. She's written squillions of yummy books, including the bestselling *Internet Girls* series and the *Eleven, Twelve,* and *Thirteen* series, and she is SO SUPER EXCITED about *Luv Ya Bunches* that she can hardly stand it. Why? Because at last she wrote a book that blends the thrills of instant messaging with the goofy, wonderful madness of fifth grade. And plus there is bobble-head turtle drama! And muddy milkshakes!! And cute yellow video cameras that capture everything!!!! (And, um, yes. She is a spaz, that Lauren. She hopes you like her anyway!)

Visit her on the web at laurenmyracle.com, and come hang with Milla, Violet, Yasaman, and Katie-Rose at LuvYaBunches.com. Unless you have, like, homework to do. Or you have to clean out your cat's litter box. Blech, hate cleaning out the litter box . . .

Mwah!